VALLEY OF GUNS

Scott Travis was an outlaw who'd been on the move too long. All he wanted was to settle down. Determined to stake a claim, he rode into Piute, Nebraska, planning one last, easy holdup.

But the town was a powder keg waiting to explode. Before Travis knew what hit him, he was in the middle of a deadly range war. To survive he would need a rancher's grit, a thief's cunning, and a gambler's luck, or the only land he'd ever own would be on Boot Hill.

VALLEY OF GUNS

Wayne D. Overholser

23-862

First published in 1955 by Ward, Lock

This hardback edition 1998
by Chivers Press
by arrangement with
Golden West Literary Agency

ISBN 0 7540 8040 4

British Library Cataloguing in Publication Data available

Chapter 1: Easy Money

THE MILES HAD LEFT THEIR MARK UPON SCOTT TRAVIS
and his black gelding, miles that stretched eastward
across the Continental Divide to the Frenchman
Valley in western Nebraska. Now, coming down
from the Broken Buttes to the grass-carpeted floor
of Easter Valley, Scott let himself dream of a drink,
a foot-long steak covered with ketchup, and a bath
if there was a tub in Piute.

Grinning wryly, Scott put the forbidden plea-
sures out of his mind. He would have none of them
today. Delazon had told him not to linger in Piute.

The road bent westward toward a group of ranch
buildings. Beyond the buildings Easter Lake made
a pale, mirrorlike oval in the distance, surrounded
by the dark green of a tule marsh. Scott left the
road, angling to his right, then turned to strike the
road from Ontario to Piute.

Delazon had drawn a map for him and given
instructions. He'd said, "Don't attract any atten-

tion after you get into Oregon. Just drift into Piute, spot the bank, and ride north. I'll see you after you leave town."

At the time Scott had considered it good advice, for there was no way a man could tell how far the Nebraska law would reach. Now that he was here, he didn't see much sense in dodging people. He wouldn't be in the valley for more than a few days at most, and then he'd be on the run again. Still, habit was a confining thing; and because he had been following Delazon's instructions he obeyed them now.

Near noon he struck the Ontario road and swung west to follow it into Piute. He was close enough to see the bright green of a line of willows that ran north and south. Remembering the map Delazon had given him, he knew this would be Talking Water Creek, the biggest stream in the valley.

Here was cowman's paradise, and it seemed strange that he had seen only one ranch in the last twenty-odd miles. It was even stranger that he had seen no cattle. The grass was stirrup-high, a vast undulating sea that swept away for miles all around him to the rimrock on the east and west, and the Blue Mountains to the north, their pine-covered ridges made hazy by distance. If the circumstances of his life had been different Scott would have liked to tarry here in Easter Valley, for it was a welcome respite from the barren emptiness that lay behind him.

The town took solid shape before him, one short business block of false-fronted buildings surrounded by dwellings, many with white picket fences and slender poplars in front. He felt a charm, a sort of friendliness that seemed to beg him to stay. He grinned at the thought. Piute would extend no welcoming hand to a drifter who had come to help rob its bank.

Scott came opposite a small house with a row of red hollyhocks along the porch. A woman was on her knees digging around them, her back to him. Sudden perverseness made him rein to a stop just outside the picket fence. He would never be able to explain to Delazon why he did it, although the explanation was simple. He was hungry for the sight of a woman's face.

He sat his saddle there at the edge of the street, one leg hooked over the horn while he rolled a cigarette. He liked the woman's slender back and her brown hair that was pinned at the base of her neck. She was young, he thought hopefully, and pretty.

Maybe she was lonely, living in a little house like this, lonely and waiting for a man to come along who looked like Scott Travis. He fired his cigarette, thinking ruefully that his week-old growth of reddish-brown stubble was enough to scare her. He should have gone into town and bought a shave and come back. But this was crazy thinking for a man who would soon be on the move again with the law on his tail.

She must have felt his presence then, for she dropped the short-handled hoe she was working with and glanced over her shoulder. He touched the brim of his hat. "Howdy, ma'am. I was just admiring that fancy crop of hollyhocks you're raising."

She stood up, brushing back a stray lock of hair that fluttered across her forehead. She was pretty, Scott saw, slender and straight-backed and quite young. Twenty-three maybe. About his age. Or younger.

"Hello." Her dark eyes were fixed questioningly on him. "Is there something I can do for you?"

He could say he just wanted to look at the hollyhocks and ride on. Probably that would be the smart thing to do. Delazon would have a fit if he knew he had stopped to talk, but right then Delazon didn't seem very important. Scott liked the looks of the woman. Nice. That was it, a nice homey woman who could probably cook a good meal.

"Why, there is something you can do for me, ma'am." He stepped down. "I was wondering if I could get a drink. A man gets mighty dry, just riding along."

She hesitated, and for an instant he had the terrible fear that she was going to tell him that, if he rode another block, he could get all the drinks he wanted. Instead she smiled and said, "Of course. Come in."

Turning, she walked into the house in quick, graceful steps. He threw his cigarette away and followed her. The front room was exactly what he had expected—wallpaper with little sailboats against a blue sea, a rag rug on the floor, two rocking chairs, a horsehair sofa, and a picture on the wall of a snow-capped mountain.

Everything was spotlessly clean. He paused, trying to remember how long it was since he had stood in a room like this. The smell of baking bread came to him from the kitchen. He swallowed. It had been a long time since he'd eaten fresh bread.

Homey, he told himself. Some women had a talent for it and some didn't. This one did. A man who shared this house with her would be lucky. He frowned, the thought occurring to him again that a man was a fool to think of things like this when he'd be trying to outrun a posse in a few days.

She had gone on into the kitchen and was working the pump that was placed at the edge of the sink along the far wall. He walked quickly to her, saying, "I guess I can pump my own drink."

She stepped back. "It will be cool if you pump a minute."

He worked the handle, water spurted into the sink. His eyes were fixed on her face, and he was thinking how women strike a man in different ways. Too many that he had known were selfish and cheap and tawdry, but this girl was clean and fine and decent. At least that was the way she impressed him. Then he wondered what sort of judgment she was making of him.

She moved to the stove and, opening the oven door, looked at her bread. She closed the door and straightened, her gaze returning to his face. He took the dipper down from the wall, filled it, and had his drink. It was cool and good, and he filled the dipper again and drank, looking over the rim at her. Flushing, she glanced away.

He hung the dipper back on the wall. "Thanks. That's good water."

"Any water's good if you're thirsty enough."

He remembered that his hat was still on his head and he took it off. She remained by the stove, waiting for him to go; but still he lingered, savoring this moment that filled him with an inward warmth he had not felt for a long time.

"Looks like a good town," he said.

"What's good about it?"

The question startled him. "Why, it just seems friendly."

"How many people have you talked to besides me?"

"None."

"Then you don't know. Are you looking for a job?"

"Maybe, if the right one comes along."

"It won't." She glanced at the walnut-handled gun on his hip and raised her gaze to his eyes, frowning. "Not if you're particular about what you do."

He guessed what was in her mind. Most women

thought the same thing. They never understood. A gun was poison to them—a notion that always puzzled him, for to his way of thinking a man was a puny thing without a gun.

"How particular?" he asked.

Her lips tightened. "Go on downtown and start asking for a job. Nobody hires a man in this country but Marvin Bengogh. He's the manager of the Northwest Land and Cattle Company."

"Maybe Bengogh's the man I'd better see."

"By all means, if you're the kind who sells his heart and soul when you hire your gun." She shook her head. "I don't know a thing about you except that you've come a long way and you were thirsty; but you don't look like Bengogh's kind of man."

"Strikes me this burg don't look so good to you," he said.

"It's not the town," she said quickly. "It's the country. I mean, some of the people who live in it."

"Nothing to do. No fun. That it?"

"No, I don't mean that at all," she cried with sudden bitterness. "It's the old story of some folks wanting to get ahead and somebody else beating them down; but I guess it's that way everywhere." She shrugged. "I shouldn't complain. I'm the teacher, and I have enough to eat. Most folks think that's all that counts."

"It helps." He sniffed audibly. "Smells good."

"My bread isn't done," she said quickly.

He grinned. "Maybe I'll be back when it is." He hesitated, trying to think of something else to say, failed, and turned toward the door. "Thanks for the drink."

She didn't say anything. When he left the house she was still there beside the stove, staring after him. He mounted and reined into the street, the thought occurring to him that she probably had her savings in the bank. Well, it was no concern of his.

She'd make out. She had her job and a place to live and enough to eat. Probably some local fellow was hounding her to marry him. Most likely she was rich. He was the one who lived in poverty.

He pulled up in front of a saloon and watered his horse at a trough, glancing along the deserted street. Across from him was a small building with the letters on a window:

Piute County Bank, Hank Nolan, Pres.

Delazon had talked as if there was a million dollars in the tin can of a safe, and all that was necessary was to walk in and throw a gun on this fellow Nolan and go out with the million dollars in his pocket.

Scott frowned as he racked his black gelding. Delazon had promised he'd have a couple more boys to help out, and three would be all the job needed. Maybe it would be as simple as he had said; but it seemed unreasonable that a bank in a two-bit burg like this would have any big amount of money, especially in the middle of summer. Roundup time maybe, but not now.

Scott rolled another cigarette and stood on the walk a moment, wondering if Delazon was in town. There was a restaurant beyond the saloon, and he turned toward it, impelled by the same perverseness that had made him stop and ask the brown-haired girl for a drink.

Before he reached the door a man stepped through it and stopped, frowning, eyes dropping to Scott's gun. Then the man moved in front of him, fingering the star on his vest. He said, "I'm Frank Hibbard. I'm the law hereabouts, and I like to keep things quiet."

"Why, now," Scott murmured, "that's fine. I like things quiet, too."

Hibbard backed up to the wall and leaned against

it, scratching his nose. He didn't look like a man who made a practice of throwing his weight around. He wasn't over thirty, but there were deep lines in his gaunt face, and his shoulders slumped as if he were completely worn out.

"Strangers don't hit this country much," he said. "Ain't no work hereabouts. Just one big outfit and it's full up right now. We've got a few little spreads north of town, but they don't hire anybody. Can't afford it."

"Maybe you could use a deputy," Scott said.

Hibbard snorted. "The county don't pay enough to keep me in bacon and beans. Well, just thought I'd tell you we don't cotton to trouble. If you're looking for a job, ride on to Crooked River. Some big layouts over there you might catch on with."

"Thanks," Scott said, and walked into the restaurant.

He took a stool at the counter and ordered a steak, wondering why the sheriff was so tired. Caught in a trap and didn't know which way to jump probably. One big outfit! He thought of what the girl had said, of some folks wanting to get ahead and somebody else beating them down. It was an old story to Scott, that he knew too well.

He wondered why anyone wanted to be sheriff in a place like this. The little fry elected him, but the big outfit told him what to do. Hibbard ought to take a look at himself some morning when he was shaving. He'd be ashamed of what he saw if he had any shame left in him.

Only one way to handle a deal like this. You kicked the big boy in the teeth, and you set him back on his heels. Then the little fellows got along. It would be as easy as that. In Hibbard's job, he'd show them, and he'd have some fun while doing it. A tough world made for tough men. Those last weeks in Nebraska had taught him that.

The counterman brought the steak and a cup of coffee, slid a ketchup bottle along the counter, and walked back into the kitchen. Scott ate with relish, asked for another cup of coffee and a dish of canned peaches, and, when he was done, lingered a moment, smoking.

The street door opened, and a big man came in. Delazon! Scott would recognize that red face if he saw it at the other end of Main Street on a dark night. Delazon called, "Murphy," and said out of the corner of his mouth as he passed Scott, "Get to hell out of town."

The counterman came out of the kitchen. "How's the cattle-buying business, Sam?"

Delazon took the stool at the far end of the counter and cuffed back his Stetson. "Bad. Bengogh won't turn loose of anything, and the little fellows can't seem to get together. I don't savvy. They claim they need money and they've got beef to sell, but they won't guarantee delivery at the railroad."

Scott slid off the stool and tossed a silver dollar on the counter, the streak of perverseness ruling him again. The deal with Delazon had seemed fair enough back in Nebraska when he had been so tired of his jail cell that anything else looked good. Now it didn't seem fair at all. Here was Delazon, big and well fed and shaved, posing as a cattle buyer. He wouldn't be taking any chances when they knocked the bank over. Hell, he wouldn't even be holding the horses.

"How about a job, mister?" Scott asked. "Buy your herd, and I'll help you drive it to the railroad."

Delazon turned to stare at him, blue eyes filled with outrage. "I never saw you before," he snapped. "I don't hire men when I don't know nothing about them."

"You ain't taking no more chances than I am,"

Scott said. "I don't know you, either."

Delazon shook his head. "I ain't hiring nobody now. I'm trying to buy a thousand head of four-year-olds, and so far I ain't been able to round up half that many. Anyhow, it'd take more'n two men to drive a herd that size to Winnemucca."

"Maybe we could rustle a few more hands," Scott said.

The counterman picked up Scott's dollar and slid his change back. "Sam, you're barking up the wrong tree. Bengogh's got the road to Winnemucca blocked. He wouldn't let five cows cross his range, let alone a thousand head."

"Yeah, that's part of the trouble," Delazon admitted. "Jay Runyan and the rest of 'em say the same thing, but I've got a hunch they just don't have the guts it takes to buck Bengogh."

Scott pocketed his change, grinning blandly at Delazon. "I ain't afraid of this Bengogh, whoever he is. You and me, mister, we'll take that herd to the railroad."

Ignoring him, Delazon said, "Cup of coffee and a slab of your mince pie, Murphy."

"Maybe I should have a recommend from my last boss," Scott said. "That it?"

Thoroughly angry now, Delazon slammed a hamlike fist on the counter, a blow that made Scott's plate rattle. "Damn it, I ain't hiring no hands. Can't you get that through your noggin?"

"You're passing up a good man, mister," Scott said, and went out, his grin widening.

For a moment he loitered in front of the restaurant, knowing he should get on his black and ride out of town; but the more he thought about it, the stronger rebellion grew in him. Funny how differently a deal like this shaped up when you had a look at it from another angle.

Delazon had it fat and easy, all right. Then

another thought came to mind. Maybe this man Bengogh who seemed to run the country had money in the bank, enough to make the job worth while. That would put a different light on the whole deal.

Scott turned toward his horse and stopped. A rider thundered into town from the south and reined up in front of the saloon, dust sweeping up around the horse in a gray cloud. The rider was a girl, the wildest-looking girl he had ever seen, her red hair falling down her back in a tangled mass.

She jumped down, looped her reins over the pole, and jerked a Winchester from the boot. She threw her head back, yelling, "Bengogh, come out here."

Chapter 2: The Big Fellow

SCOTT WAS NEVER ONE TO MOVE ON WHEN HE SAW ANY-thing that looked like fun, and this promised plenty. The girl was not more than eighteen, he judged, small and freckled and undoubtedly the angriest person he had ever seen. She was wearing a tan riding-skirt and a man's blue shirt that was open at the throat. She stood sideways to him, her round breasts rising and falling as anger boiled higher in her.

Men came out of the saloon, a small, swarthy man in front who gave the girl a friendly smile. He asked, "You wanted to see me, Patsy?"

He had a well-shaved, bay-rum look, his black mustache was carefully trimmed, and his clothes were expensive and immaculate. In spite of his short stature and banty-rooster pride, he contrived to give the impression that he was an important man. This, Scott thought, would be Marvin Bengogh.

The girl wadded up a sheet of paper and threw it at him. "No, I don't want to see you," she cried. "Just answer one question. Did you write that?"

Stooping, Bengogh picked the paper up, flattened it out, and glanced at it. "Yes, I wrote it, Patsy. You know I have to carry out orders that come to me, and I've already given you six weeks more than I—"

"Sure, I've heard that song and dance till I'm sick of it," the girl shouted. "You carry out the orders Alec Schmidt gives you, so nobody's supposed to blame you. Well, I don't see your Alec Schmidt, so you'll have to do until he comes along."

Suddenly Scott realized the girl aimed to kill Bengogh. She brought the Winchester to her shoulder and thumbed back the hammer. Other men, attracted by the commotion, were drifting along the walk, and Sheriff Hibbard called out in a frantic tone, "Patsy! Don't do it, Patsy."

Scott was the closest to her. He lunged forward and knocked the rifle barrel up just as the girl pulled the trigger. The bullet sliced through the front of the saloon five feet over Bengogh's head, then Scott twisted the Winchester out of the girl's hands.

She whirled on him like an infuriated wildcat, small fists hammering his face. He dropped the rifle and got an arm around her, trying to smother her blows. She hit him on the nose with a surprisingly strong punch for so small a girl, then he had both of her wrists in his hands and held her helpless.

"You oughtta let a man do jobs like that for you," he said.

"A man," she screamed. "What man? If there was a man in this valley he'd have blowed

Bengogh's head off six months ago."

"So you want a man," Scott said. "If I'd known that, I'd have got here sooner."

Bengogh laughed easily. He said, "Thanks, friend. Drop out to the ranch sometime, and I'll pay you for your trouble. Patsy, I've made you a fair offer. I'll be disappointed in you if you don't accept it after you cool off." Turning, he walked back into the saloon, apparently unruffled by an incident which could easily have caused his death.

The crowd did not scatter. The girl began to cry, and Scott dropped her wrists. He said softly, "I'm sorry, but tomorrow you'll thank me."

Hibbard stepped up, saying in a hopeful voice, "All right, boys. The drinks are on me."

Still the crowd remained, townsmen and the buckaroos who had followed Bengogh out of the saloon. Some were Mexican vaqueros who had probably come to the valley from Nevada or California, perhaps with Bengogh. One of the buckaroos strode across to Hibbard, saying in a peremptory voice, "Arrest her, sheriff. If that wasn't a good try at murder, I never saw one."

Scott took one look at the fellow, tall and lanky with a tobacco-stained mustache and a gun belted low on his right hip. *Bengogh's man,* Scott thought. He said quietly, "I'm a stranger here, but it don't take long to smell skunk smell when you're close to the skunk. Maybe the girl's had the stink in her nose so long she couldn't stand it no longer."

"No trouble, now," Hibbard said in his tired voice. "I ain't arresting her." He nodded at Patsy. "Git for home."

"Home!" She brought a sleeve across her eyes, blinked, and stamped a foot. "What home is there for me to go to?"

"You can stay with Sally—" Hibbard began.

"You said home." The girl motioned to the paper

Bengogh had dropped on the walk. "Look at what that ornery son wrote and stuck on my door. I don't even have the home I've lived in for the last five years. He wants me to come and work in his house. That's the offer he made. What does he think I am? A floozy he can—"

The lanky man crowded closer to her. "None of that. He offered you a home because he felt sorry for you, and if you had a lick of sense in your red head you'd take him up on it."

"I know what he is, Tally," the girl cried bitterly. "You're no better. I wouldn't trust either one of you with a pet coon. You're both liars and thieves and—"

Tally swung an open palm at the girl's cheek. She ducked and would have waded in with her fists swinging if Scott hadn't moved faster. He started the punch below his belt; he caught Tally on the side of the head and knocked him flat on his back.

The girl scooped up the Winchester Scott had dropped, screaming, "Kane, keep your hands off your guns, or I'll let daylight through you."

Scott glimpsed the long-haired kid standing in front of the batwings, then had no time to see anyone except Tally, for the lanky man had scrambled to his feet and was moving in. For a time his hands were full. He met Tally's rush, swapping blow for blow; he was smaller, with a shorter reach, and for a moment he was at a disadvantage.

Scott backed up, ducking and pivoting and taking most of Tally's punches on his elbows and shoulders. Then he reversed himself and carried the fight to Tally. He took one of Tally's windmill blows in the chest; he ducked another wild swing and then he was in close: he whipped a right to Tally's mouth that brought a gush of blood from a split lip. Tally, caught off balance, went down again.

The girl was jumping up and down, screaming,

"Give it to him, stranger. Knock hell out of him."

The buckaroos standing beside the long-haired kid in front of the batwings were yelling for Tally to get up. Tally, momentarily dazed, took his time. He raised himself on an elbow and wiped a hand across his face, smearing the blood until it was a red mask, then he came on up off the walk and dived headlong at Scott.

Scott clubbed him on the side of the head with a right, but it didn't stop Tally's rush. He got his arms around Scott, the impetus of his charge carrying them both off the walk into the street dust at the end of the hitchpole. Scott fell on his back, and Tally brought his head down into Scott's belly, knocking the wind out of him.

Scott got an arm around the back of Tally's head, hugging him so he couldn't butt him again. They rolled over, dust rising around them in a thick, choking cloud. Scott held his grip around Tally's head with his left arm; he swung his right into the fellow's ribs, but it was not an effective blow. They went on over again, threshing and kicking, and Scott got him in the side again, knocking a grunt out of him and hurting him enough to make him relax his grip. Scott tore loose and, regaining his feet, backed into the street.

"Come on," the girl was screaming. "Come on, stranger. You've got to take him."

Her words beat at Scott's ears; he heard the rumble of men's voices, and through the red haze of fury that swept across his vision he made sense out of what the girl said. "You've got to take him." Time was running out for him. The girl might not be able to hold the crowd off.

Tally came up out of the dust, blood dribbling from the cut lip, and Scott moved in fast, driven by the urge to end this. Tally struck out, but he was a little slow, and Scott ducked and closed with him, hitting him with his right and then his left, hard blows that rocked Tally's head one way and then the other, the sound as solid as that of a butcher's cleaver on a side of beef.

Tally's eyes were glazed, the power gone out of him. Fighting now by instinct, he swung again, a clublike blow that fanned Scott's jaw. Tally, off balance, was wide open, and Scott sledged him squarely on the point of the chin. That was all. His knees folded, and he went down in a slow, curling drop, and lay still.

Scott took a long, deep breath and wiped a hand across his face. He heard a whisper of movement from the crowd, heard the girl cry, "Stand pat. I'll kill the first one who makes a wrong move." And Hibbard: "Easy, Patsy, easy."

Scott walked to the horse trough and sloshed water over his face; he wiped his hands on his pants and looked at the crowd, knowing that he'd asked for trouble and beating Tally into the dust might not be the end of it.

"Bengogh own you, too?" Scott asked, fixing his eyes on the long-haired kid.

"Nobody owns me," the kid breathed. "I'm Jimmy Kane. That mean anything to you?"

"Not a damned thing," Scott said. "Want some of what I gave your partner?"

The kid laughed, lips springing away from yellow teeth. "I told you I was Jimmy Kane." He patted the butts of his guns. "Jimmy Kane don't get down on the ground and roll around like a schoolboy."

"No more trouble, now," Hibbard said, his voice more tired-sounding than ever. "I'll run you in if you start anything else."

The kid laughed again, an ugly jeering sound. "Frank, you never saw the day you could run me anywhere." He brought his pale eyes to Scott. "Friend, this country is too hot for you. Slope out before you get burned." Turning, he pushed through the swing doors into the saloon.

Hibbard took a ragged breath. He said to one of the buckaroos, "Tote Wick inside. The fun's over."

"It just started, Frank," the man said. "When we was riding in this morning, Jimmy and Wick told Marvin he'd been too easy. I reckon he'll believe 'em now."

They picked Tally up and carried him inside, the rest of the buckaroos following. Relieved, Hibbard turned to the girl. "Get along, now. Your daddy was always a trouble-maker, and you ain't no better."

The girl didn't hear him. She was staring at Scott, her Winchester lowered. "Mister," she said reverently, "there is a man in town."

He winked at her, then turned his gaze to the townsmen who were backing away. "Lots of pants around here, but I don't see none of 'em that have got men inside 'em."

They walked away, red-faced, ashamed, and hating him because he had pinned that shame upon them. Hibbard shook his head, glaring at Scott. He said, "I don't know who you are or where you came from or why you're here, but Jimmy Kane was right. This country's too hot for you. You'd best drift."

"No hurry," Scott said. "You claim you like it quiet. Looks to me like you're gonna have a rough time keeping it that way. You're gonna need some help."

"Not from you." Hibbard leaned against the hitchpole. "It's been quiet except when Patsy's dad raised hell. Now slope along."

Scott turned to the girl, who had slid her Winchester into the scabbard. "He wants us to drift."

"Then we'd better do it," she said, and swung into the saddle.

Scott moved to his black. As he mounted he saw

Delazon in front of the restaurant, glaring at him.
Scott winked, and reined into the street, wondering
what Delazon would say when he had a chance to
talk. Well, it didn't make a hell of a lot of difference. He had no regret for what he had done. If
Delazon didn't like it, he would keep on riding.
Chances were, that bank safe wasn't worth cracking
anyhow.

Chapter 3: The Girl Patsy

They took the south road out of town, the girl
eyeing Scott with a frank admiration that embarrassed him. She said nothing until they were out on
the grass, the road a faint mark on the level floor of
the valley. Then she held out a brown little hand.
"I'm Patsy Clark," she said. "I want to shake hands
with a man ten feet tall."

"You're cutting that a little long." He gripped her
hand, finding it hard with calluses. "I'm Scott
Travis."

"No, sir, you're not an inch under ten feet," she
said. "I don't know where you're headed, and
chances are you wouldn't tell me if I asked; but one
thing's sure. You'd better start for wherever you're
going."

"I ain't in no big hurry."

"You look like you've come a ways," she said.

"Yeah, quite a ways." He thought of Delazon and
frowned. "Maybe this would be a good place to
light and rest."

"Yeah, if you like resting on top of a volcano.
That's what we've got here."

"What was that paper you threw at Bengogh?"

"A notice to get out of my cabin," the girl said bitterly. "The company owns the land, or so it claims. Ever hear of the Cascade and Malheur Wagon Road Company?"

"No."

"Not many people have. They sure didn't build a road. Just drove some stakes through the sagebrush and then ran a wagon between the stakes. It was enough to give them the land, though. Bengogh's had everybody evicted who lived south of what he calls the boundary except me. He let me stay because my mother was dying. Buried her last week. Now he says I've got to get out."

"Real considerate," Scott murmured, "letting you stay this long."

"I've wondered about that," the girl said thoughtfully. "Bengogh doesn't do considerate things. You see, the road company got title to alternate sections of land. The other sections still belong to the government and are legally open to entry. Since I'm the only one who wasn't evicted, I've got a hunch my quarter doesn't belong to the company."

"Legally, you say." Scott grinned. "I reckon that's a word Bengogh don't worry about."

She nodded. "Nobody has really tried to find out because they're afraid of him. Bengogh claims all of it, and with toughs like Wick Tally and Jimmy Kane backing him up, he's sitting real pretty."

"Is his company the outfit that first got the road grant?"

She shook her head. "The grant was made years ago, but at that time the land wasn't worth anything because the Piutes were ornery and nobody wanted to settle here. After the Indians were corralled, a few families drifted into the valley, including mine. Then Bengogh showed up with a crew and a herd of heifers and claimed the Northwest Land and Cattle

Company had bought the road grant."

"Who's this Alec Schmidt you mentioned?"

"An old Dutchman who built up a big cattle business in California, then spread into Nevada and finally got up here. He owns several ranches along the Malheur, but I guess his other managers aren't like Bengogh."

They rode in silence for a time. The red fury that the fight with Tally had aroused in Scott began to die, and he wished he hadn't got tangled up in the girl's troubles. Still he knew he'd do exactly the same thing if he had the last hour to live over. He was not, he thought wryly, as inconsistent as that most of the time.

The thing to do was see that she got safely to her cabin; then he'd go back, swing around Piute, and ride north. Delazon would be waiting somewhere along the trail. He'd see what the man had to say. If Delazon was too horny, he would say to hell with the whole business and ride on.

They left the road and crossed the creek, a slow, meandering stream, and angled southwest toward the lake. The ground was soft under their horses' hoofs, the grass belly-high, and again Scott was struck with the thought that here was a cowman's paradise with the cows missing. A good place to stay, he thought with growing bitterness; but a man didn't knock a bank over and then settle down within a few miles of the bank.

He glanced sideways at Patsy, who was staring straight ahead, her face shadowed by bitterness. He asked, "Where does Bengogh run the company cattle?"

She glanced at him, startled, and it took a moment to lift her mind from the sour rut her thoughts had fallen into. She motioned across the lake. "He keeps the she stuff and calves yonder in the southeast corner of the valley. The steers are farther south in the Steens. Come fall, he'll fetch the steers back and winter them in the valley."

"How many does he run?"

"About five thousand head. The gossip is that Schmidt will be in the valley before long, and Bengogh claims that when the old man gets a look at the grass he'll double the size of the herd. I guess this ranch is doing better than the rest of Schmidt's outfits."

They were following the edge of the marsh. A flock of mallards flew overhead, coming in low and settling in the open water beyond the tules. An avocet took wing ahead of Scott and the girl, making the air sad with its melancholy cry. A crane stood on one stiltlike leg, eyeing them.

The wind, blowing in off the lake, was cool and damp and laden with marsh smell. Scott had seen many lakes in the sand hills of western Nebraska, but they were mere puddles cupped between the ridges. Here the world seemed made up of sky and marsh and lake, the Broken Buttes to the south a vague line against the horizon.

This was a wild and massive land, a strange, new land to Scott, stretching out for miles under a brilliant sky, the grass moving in long, sweeping waves before the wind. He thought of his own rootless past, of an unnamed feeling that had been in him as long as he could remember, and again it seemed to him that this was where he would like to stay. Now the feeling grew and warmed him, and he found himself thinking of the dark-haired girl who had given him a drink.

He shook his head, telling himself he was the last man on earth who should be permitting himself the luxury of dreams like that. He said, "Quite a country."

"I love it," Patsy said softly. "For poor people like we were, it's as close to heaven as you can get.

Even if we lost our calf crop, we still could get a living from the lake and the creek. I've heard Dad say that a thousand times."

"He's not alive?"

She shook her head, bleak eyes on the cabin that was directly ahead of them. "He was killed last spring. Ma and me had been visiting the Vances. When we got home we found him in the corral with one side of his head smashed in. He was breaking a bad horse, so it was easy for Hibbard to say the horse killed him, but I know he was murdered."

"What about your mother?"

"She just didn't want to live after we found Dad. I suppose no doctor would agree with me, but I say she died of a broken heart. She and Dad were terribly in love." She bit her lower lip, then added in a whisper, "It was wonderful to see them. They never let their love die like so many people do."

He thought of Bengogh, of futile Frank Hibbard, of Delazon, and he hated all of them. It was a tough world, a dirty, stinking world that let men like Bengogh run things and smother life from people. He knew now what the dark-haired girl had meant when she'd said, "It's the old story of some folks wanting to get ahead and somebody else beating them down." But it had always been that way. You could find the same story wherever you went, and there was nothing Scott could do about changing it.

He asked, "Where were you when Bengogh left that notice for you to get out?"

"I rode up to the Vances' to ask George if he'd buy my hens. When I got back the notice was tacked on my door. I went to the company ranch, but Bengogh was gone; so I figured I'd find him in town." She glanced at Scott, a sudden humility in her. "I'm sorry I hit you."

Scott rubbed his nose ruefully. "Quite a poke. About as good as anything Tally landed."

"I'm sorry," she said. "That's all I can say."

They reached the cabin and reined up. He started to tell her he'd be riding on now, but before he could speak she said, "Somehow I'll make it up to you. I'll get a few things and be right out."

He knew that he looked ridiculous, his mouth sagging open as the full significance of her words struck him. She'd attached herself to him, which to all intents and purposes meant he'd adopted her, a redheaded, fiery-tempered girl who had tried to kill a man and had hit him on the nose and made it hurt like an ulcerated tooth. She stepped down and ran into the cabin, while he stared blankly after her and wondered how he was going to get out of this.

He rolled a cigarette, considering what he'd say to her when she came back. He couldn't tell her about Delazon, or that if he went ahead on the bank deal he'd be traveling fast and far in a few days. Maybe he could tell her he was drifting through the country looking for a riding job but, after what had happened in town, he couldn't get one here. He'd fixed himself when he'd bought into her trouble. Sure, that would do. She'd make out. But he knew she wouldn't. Not against a man like Bengogh.

Scott hooked a leg over the saddle horn and glanced around. The cabin was small and built of logs, probably hauled from the Blue Mountains; and that had been quite a haul. There was a shed and some stockade corrals, the first he'd seen, built by setting juniper posts close together in a trench and lacing willows between them.

Directly behind the house he could see a garden with cabbage and turnips and carrots, the hardy vegetables that would grow here where the summers were short and the winters hard. An uneasiness began to nag him as he stared at the straight, neat rows. He couldn't see a weed anywhere, and the heavy soil had been carefully tilled—hard work for a girl. Then he remembered the calluses on her hand. She had counted on this garden to get her through the winter. She had courage, the dogged, stubborn courage that he admired in either man or woman.

He saw the graves to the left of the garden, a small, tight fence around them; and something seemed to fill his chest and tighten his throat. All that Patsy Clark wanted was a chance to live here in peace. Now she was running because she knew she couldn't fight Marvin Bengogh alone. Scott sat his saddle, staring at the graves, and he cursed Bengogh in a low, bitter voice.

Patsy ran out of the cabin, a half-filled flour sack in her hand, her head bowed so that he would not see her tears. Smoke drifted through the door, and he knew what she had done. She had fired the only place she could call home because she could not let Bengogh have it.

With quick, deft motions she tied the sack behind her saddle and stepped up. Then he saw her face and something happened to him. He couldn't desert her. He'd have to take her along when he left the valley, a redheaded orphan who trusted a man because he'd taken chips in her fight.

She swung her horse and rode away, saying nothing until they were half a mile from the cabin. He looked back once and saw that flames had eaten through the roof; but Patsy stared straight ahead. Then they topped a rise and there was just the smoke from the burning cabin behind them, a stain on the horizon.

"We'll stay off the road," Patsy said. "We don't want to run into Bengogh and his bunch going back to the company ranch."

They swung north, keeping the willows along the creek between them and the road. Presently she said, "I sold all my cows and my other horse to Jay

Runyan because I had to have some money when Ma died and I owed a big bill at the store. I don't have anything left but my hens. George Vance will come and get them. He's not afraid of Bengogh."

They rode in silence for a time, and doubts began to plague Scott as he thought of Delazon and the men who would be waiting for him north of Piute. A few moments before he had made up his mind to take the girl with him. Now it seemed a crazy thing to do.

"Them Vances you mentioned," Scott said. "You'll want to go there—"

"I can't," she said sharply. "They don't have enough to eat now. A whole batch of kids. If George goes hunting and doesn't get anything, they're hungry. I'd just be another mouth to feed." She glanced briefly at him. "They were our neighbors on the lake before Bengogh evicted them. George could always fetch in a goose or some ducks, but he's too far away now. He's got a few cows, but he settled on an awfully poor piece of graze. He'll wind up broke as sure as shooting."

"Hibbard said something about you staying with Sally."

"He meant Sally Runyan. She's the teacher in Piute. I can't live with her, either. She saves every penny she can to help Frank Hibbard buy a business when his term's done. They're engaged."

"Engaged!" He stared at her, the word jolted out of him. This Sally Runyan must be the dark-haired girl who had given him a drink. She'd said she was the teacher. "She can't be engaged to that tin-star toter."

"What do you know about Sally?"

"I stopped at her place for a drink when I rode into town."

"Oh! Well, she's engaged, all right, and everybody's like you. They wonder why. I guess it's like Dad used to say. You never know why a woman falls in love with a man."

He looked ahead at the grass, swept by the wind in long, ceaseless waves. That proved he was a knucklehead for thinking about a girl after he'd seen her once. Sure, she was pretty and nice and homey, the kind of girl he wanted, but not if she saw anything in a no-good like Frank Hibbard.

"There must be somebody—" he began.

"You." She reined up, the corners of her mouth quivering. "Mister, Dad always said that if a man took to stray pups and kids you could trust him. I'm eighteen, old enough to be a woman; but I guess I'm still a kid, or I wouldn't have done a fool trick like going after Bengogh."

He had pulled his black to a stop, eyes on the girl's taut face. "I reckon you'll grow up."

"I'm starting right now. You've got to take me with you. I can't stay here." She swallowed. "I tell you I'll make it up. Some way."

"I'm just a drifter. You can't live like I do."

"I'm used to getting along on mighty little." She put a hand to her throat, her eyes begging him. "If I stay here I'll wind up shooting Bengogh, and they'll hang me. I've got to get out of the country, and a girl can't travel alone."

He kept looking at her, thinking of the graves and her garden, of the cabin she'd burned. Well, he was licked. He had a heart as soft as a custard pudding and he'd always prided himself on being as tough as the next one, but he was licked.

"All right," he said. "I guess we'd best get along. I've got to meet some men north of town."

She gave him a quick smile. "Mister, I love you."

"Now, hold on—"

"I didn't mean it that way." She lowered her gaze, blushing. "I meant you're pretty wonderful, letting me tag along. I don't know what you're up to; but, whatever it is, I'll help."

They rode on, Scott thinking glumly of Delazon. She could help. Sure, she could hold the horses while he knocked over that bank. That would fix everything up fine, getting her tangled up in a bank-robbing job, just fine. He was a knucklehead for sure.

Chapter 4: The Whisper of Doubt

SALLY RUNYAN DID NOT MOVE FROM WHERE SHE STOOD beside the stove until the stranger had mounted and ridden down the street. Her conscience hurt her as she stooped and lifted the bread pan from the oven. She'd lied to him about the bread not being done. She'd been uneasy, with a man she had never seen before standing here in her kitchen and looking at her with a sort of reverence as if she were an angel or a goddess. She was far from either. At this moment she felt downright wicked.

She took the loaves of bread from the pan and put them on the table to cool. She could have brought milk and butter out of the pantry and fed him. He'd have liked her bread. Everybody did. She was the best cook in Easter Valley, or so Frank Hibbard claimed; and that was one thing Frank said she wanted to believe.

The stranger had a hungry look about him. He'd probably been on the trail for weeks, eating camp grub until he was sick of it. She walked to the stove and stood with her back to it; the knowledge that work waited to be done nagged her, but she remained there, picturing the stranger's face, the reddish-brown stubble, the wide nose and broad chin and gray eyes.

She couldn't forget his eyes. Friendly eyes like those of an affection-starved pup. No, that wasn't it. Friendly eyes, all right, but they were the eyes of a man who was looking at something pleasant he had not expected to see. She remembered that both the horse and the rider looked as if they had come a long way. He hadn't told her anything about himself. Not even his name.

She picked up a bucket and, pumping it full, carried it through the back door to her garden. She dribbled it along a row of carrots, realizing that the hot wind yesterday had dried the ground out. If it didn't rain soon, she'd have a lot of watering to do.

Frank wasn't much help. It irritated her to think of that. He just walked around town, carrying his star as if it exempted him from work. He was tired, he'd say, if she mentioned there was wood to be cut, or hoeing in the garden; but he was always on hand if there was something to eat.

Now as so many times before, this last year, she considered what her life would be like if she were married to Frank Hibbard. They had been engaged for more than two years, so that she thought about their future as a matter of habit. Her brother Jay didn't like Frank and made no secret of it. He asked every time he saw her, "Why don't you marry the fellow if you're going to?" She couldn't answer. It was just that Frank was always evasive when she mentioned getting married.

She understood, or tried to make herself think she did. Frank wanted to start a feed store here in Piute, but there weren't enough people in the valley to make it pay. Besides, he didn't have five hundred dollars to his name. She didn't have much more than that, but they kept saving. Maybe by the time his term as sheriff was over they'd have enough. Perhaps more people would be living in the valley, too.

The irritation grew in her as she took the bucket back into the kitchen and left it under the sink. She went out through the front and, picking up the hoe she had dropped, began working in the hollyhocks again. Frank was too careful. That was the trouble. He should never have taken the sheriff's star in the first place; but the job paid better than riding for Marvin Bengogh, and there was no other choice.

Then her mind turned again to the stranger. She could not help feeling ashamed when she mentally admitted she had been attracted by him. He wasn't big. He certainly wasn't handsome. Still, there was something about him she liked. Perhaps it was that strange feeling of reverence she imagined she had sensed in him.

Imagined! That was probably it. Maybe there was something in the back of his mind behind those gray eyes that would have shocked her if she had known. Most men were that way when they looked at a woman. At least that was what her brother Jay said, and she could believe it.

Frank insisted that standing up in front of a preacher was just a formality. It didn't mean anything if two people loved each other. That kind of talk irritated her more than anything else Frank did or said. He wanted all that marriage gave a man without any of the responsibilities.

She didn't want to think the stranger had ideas like that when he had looked at her. She kept digging, wondering what there was about the dusty newcomer that had aroused her interest. He had a nice smile that went all the way up into his eyes, and there was a sort of go-to-hell look about him that she liked, as if there wasn't anything he was afraid to tackle.

If only Frank had a little more of that look! If he just had the courage to tell Bengogh he couldn't go on keeping people off land that didn't belong to the company. But Frank didn't. He went right on talking soft and walking easy and being tired.

She heard a shot from downtown and ran into the street. There was a crowd in front of the saloon, but it was too far away to make out who the men were. She went back to her digging, thinking bleakly that Frank was probably talking about keeping things quiet. Then she was ashamed. He might have been hurt. No, somebody would have come for her if he had been.

She went around the house to her garden and, kneeling beside the carrots, began to pull weeds. It would be at least another month before the carrots were big enough to eat. So far she'd had nothing from the garden except some radishes and peas. Another month of battling the weeds and carrying water and hoeing. Then more of the same if she was going to have enough carrots to put away in the cellar.

It struck her suddenly that she was hungry and she had forgotten to cook dinner. Returning to the kitchen, she built up the fire. She broke an egg into a dish and put bacon on to fry, the loneliness in her making an ache in her heart. If she could just see some hope for their future! Here she was, getting older every day, with other men staying away from her because of Frank, and he hadn't even bought an engagement ring.

She heard his steps on the front porch and turned from the stove as he came in the way he usually did, without knocking. He said, "Morning, Sally," took off his hat, and sat down at the table, so tired he slumped in his chair. She went back into the pantry for another egg, thinking he must have smelled the bacon. It wasn't morning now, not to anyone but Frank who usually slept late, and at that moment she thought she hated him.

"What happened downtown?" she asked, her back to him.

"Bengogh gave Patsy notice to get out of her cabin, and she rode into town to kill him."

Sally whirled from the stove. "I heard a shot."

Hibbard nodded. "Patsy was going to blow Bengogh's head off, but there's a tough stranger in town. He saved Bengogh's hide by knocking her rifle up."

Turning back to the stove, she forked the bacon out of the frying-pan and slid the eggs into the grease. "He should have let her kill Bengogh."

"No," Hibbard said with more sharpness than his voice usually held. "I'd have had to arrest Patsy if she'd killed him. It'd be a bad proposition."

That was true. Sally spooned grease over the eggs, certain that Frank was thinking less of Patsy's welfare than he was of his own troubles that would have followed Bengogh's killing. She asked, "What happened to the stranger?"

Hibbard grinned wryly. "Made quite a splurge. Wick Tally tried to make me arrest Patsy, but I wouldn't do it. Then he got into a fight with the stranger and got licked. Knocked colder'n a piece of salt side. Jimmy started talking tough, and the stranger faced him down. Then he rode off with Patsy."

Sally took the eggs out of the frying-pan and set the platter with the eggs and bacon on the table. She brought two plates from the pantry and slid one before Hibbard; she pumped a pitcher of water and went back into the pantry for cups. Then she pulled up a chair and sat down, hoping Frank would not sense the emotion that was warming her. No one had knocked Wick Tally out in a fight since he had come to the valley, and no one had faced young Kane down.

"Anybody know who he is?" she asked, trying to make it sound as if she were only slightly interested.

Hibbard reached for a loaf of bread, tore off a big piece, and spread butter thickly over it. "No. Just rode in and rode off. I sure hope he keeps going. If he don't, we'll have trouble as sure as I'm a foot high."

"You've already got trouble," she said irritably. "When are you going to make a law-abiding man out of Bengogh?"

He had just crammed his mouth full of fresh bread, and now he almost choked, his eyes wide as he stared at Sally. He struggled with the bread for a moment, gulped, and took a drink of water. "You want me to commit suicide?"

"I want you to be sheriff. That's all."

"You'd think I had some life insurance made out in your name," he muttered, his eyes on his plate. "Might as well shoot myself as start bucking the Northwest Land and Cattle Company." He looked up, adding defensively, "Besides, nobody wants to move onto their range that I know of."

She picked up her fork and toyed with a piece of bacon. "Frank, if this valley was settled like it ought to be, you'd have a good chance to make a go of your feed store. Have you thought of that?"

"Sure I have," he muttered. "But it ain't my business to see that folks come here to settle. There's enough land in the north half of the valley anyhow for them that wants it."

"Not the best land," she said.

"Good enough."

Suddenly she wasn't hungry. She pushed her

plate toward Hibbard, asking, "Can you eat my egg?"

"Sure." He reached for it and slid it and the bacon into his plate. "Lose your appetite?"

"I guess so. Frank, are we going to get married or not?"

He put his fork down and licked his lips, a yellow smear of egg yolk remaining on the corner of his mouth. "Are we going through that again?"

"Yes."

"You know as well as I do that we can't get married on what I make. When we get enough saved—"

"By that time I'll be too old to have a baby. I'm a little tired, Frank, tired of waiting."

"Just as well if we don't have any babies," he said grumpily. "Look at George Vance. His wife has a baby every spring regular as the calendar rolls around. He won't get ahead, no matter—"

"But they're happy," Sally cried. "I've been in their home, and I know. They laugh a lot. Joke all the time. I'd rather live that way and not have anything than live the way I'm living."

He went on eating, his face shadowed by bitterness. "I know what you're thinking, Sally. Just seems that I've got bad luck all the time. I guess I'll rob Nolan's bank, or take my savings and get into a poker game."

She laughed uncertainly. One idea was as preposterous as the other. "I guess you won't do any such thing. I don't mind teaching. I was thinking about this stranger. If he does stay in the country, he might start folks thinking that Bengogh can be licked."

"If your brother had any gumption—"

"Jay says that about you, Frank."

"Why, that ain't fair. I'm the sheriff, and the sheriff has got to see that property is protected.

After all, the company did buy the wagon-road grant; and I aim to see their rights are protected. It's different with Jay. Folks look up to him because he's well fixed."

"But he wasn't evicted. That's why he says he hasn't got any fight with Bengogh." Sally leaned forward. "Frank, I'm going to write to the governor. We've got to do something about Bengogh closing the road to Winnemucca and keeping folks off government land."

He reared back in his chair, frightened. "No, you don't. We ain't kicking up any fuss if we can help it."

She rose. "Bengogh's breaking the law. I'm going to write that letter, and then I'm going to the Triangle R. I'll ask Jay if he'll loan me the money to start your feed store."

"You think he will?" Hibbard asked eagerly.

She had thought about asking Jay for a long time, but she had lacked the courage because she was reasonably sure he would turn her down. Now she knew she had to find out.

"I don't know." She filled the firebox and set the teakettle on the front of the stove. "When the water gets hot, you wash and dry the dishes and put them away. I'll write that letter and mail it, and then I'll go."

Hibbard leaned back in his chair and filled his pipe with tobacco that he carried loose in his coat pocket, his face showing his hurt. "Doing dishes is woman's work, and I ain't no woman."

"Writing this letter is a man's job," she snapped, "and I'm not a man."

She walked into the living-room, leaving him sitting there, looking picked at. She found paper and pen and ink and sat down at her desk. For several minutes she remained motionless, thinking about what to write, and then for a quarter of an hour there was no sound but the steady scratching of her pen.

She sealed and stamped the envelope and, stepping into her bedroom, changed to a blouse, riding-skirt, and boots. She put on her wide-brimmed hat, tightened the chin strap, and went into the kitchen. The fire had burned low, the teakettle was singing, and Hibbard was sitting where she had left him, pulling steadily on his pipe.

"It ain't right for a man to do dishes," he began argumentatively. "Now if we was married—"

"Frank, I want to tell you something. We'll never be married if you don't quit dragging your heels. I'm staying with Jay tonight. The garden has to be watered, the carrots need weeding, and there's some hoeing to be done. I want it all finished before I get back. You'll have to milk the cow and feed the chickens, too."

She walked out, her head held high. She could still hear his sputtering when she reached the barn. This was the first time she had ever talked to Frank that way, she thought as she saddled her bay mare. She should have made it plain a long time ago that the man she married was going to work. He'd been dragging his heels too long. Then suddenly it struck her that everything between them depended on whether he did the chores she had left for him.

She rode by the post office and mailed the letter, thinking that Frank wasn't the only one who had been dragging his heels. They were all guilty. She had shut her eyes to what Bengogh had done because she hadn't known what to do, and now she wasn't sure this letter would accomplish what she hoped it would. Jay was worse because he could have done something.

No, they were all guilty, she told herself as she took the north road out of town. All of them except George Vance, who had tried to organize the small

ranchers at the time they were being evicted and
had failed. Pat Clark, too, before he had been
killed.

She wished with a growing sense of guilt that she
had not thought about Pat Clark. She was sure that
he had been murdered, just as Patsy said. Frank's
dismissal of his death as an accident had been a
little too simple. She had a bad moment as she
asked herself if Frank had taken the easy way out as
he so often had. Then she felt something that was
close to panic. Suppose he had? She could never
marry a man like that.

Chapter 5: Fraud

THE SUN HAD SWUNG OVER TOWARD THE WESTERN RIM
when Scott and Patsy reached a road that ran east
and west across the valley. Piute lay to their right, a
huddle of buildings set out there in the center of the
valley floor. From here it seemed no larger than a
toy town.

"Where does this road go?" Scott asked.

"Prineville. You'd take it if you were going to the
Columbia."

They angled toward the creek, Scott saying easily, "Well, I ain't going to the Columbia."

They were silent again, Patsy glancing at him
occasionally, but refusing to ask the question that
Scott knew was in her mind. It was just as well. He
didn't like girls who let their tongues wag over
every impulse that struck their minds. Besides, he
needed time to think.

Delazon would be up here somewhere, and he
had said he'd have two men on hand to help with

the bank deal. Chances were, those men would be hardcases who had been robbing banks since they were big enough to fork a horse. They'd get wrong ideas the minute they laid their eyes on Patsy. Nothing like a woman to bring out the bad in some men, and Patsy was the kind who could bring out the bad in a good man if she set her mind to it.

For some reason Scott's thoughts turned again to Sally Runyan, and he was remembering that Patsy had said she was engaged to Frank Hibbard. That was a hell of a thing, the way he looked at it. Hibbard was so tired he'd go to sleep in his chair right after supper every night.

If Scott stayed in the country, he'd see about that engagement between Sally and Hibbard. He wondered what Patsy would think about that, and glanced at her pert, freckled face. The man who married her wouldn't go to sleep after supper. Not right away anyhow.

They splashed across the creek, a swift, clear stream at this point, chattering noisily as it pounded southward toward the floor of the valley. The country was lifting now, the first small pines on a low ridge ahead of them. They turned north to follow the road that paralleled the creek, Scott asking, "Where does this go?"

"Into the mountains. There are a few ranches up here." She motioned toward a group of buildings a mile or more from the road. "That's Triangle R, Jay Runyan's spread. He settled up here before we came to the valley, figuring everybody else would take land along the lake." She laughed shortly. "He guessed right, but now he's got neighbors. He can thank Bengogh for that."

"Any relation to the teacher?"

"Brother." She scowled, staring at the Triangle R buildings. "He's one man who could make trouble for Bengogh if he wanted to."

Scott looked at her curiously. "Why is he any different than anybody else?"

"Because he's got money," she said bitterly. "I guess most people are just feeble-minded. Dad and George Vance wanted to fight Bengogh when he started evicting everybody, but nobody would pay any attention to them. They were like the rest. Didn't have anything."

"What's having money got to do with it?"

"Folks respect Jay and listen to him. They say he got ahead. He's smart. Even Bengogh is friendly to him." She gestured wearily. "I'm just trying to say that Jay could be a leader if he wanted to."

"Does his sister come up here?"

"Once in a while." Patsy smiled. "One of these days Sally and Jay are going to have a whopper of a fight over Frank Hibbard. Jay says he's the biggest failure in the country; but you know how women are."

"Don't reckon I do."

"I mean a woman can't see anything wrong with a man until after they're married, and then she spends the rest of her life wishing she'd never seen him." She frowned thoughtfully. "I don't know about Sally, though. Sometimes she acts like she's about done waiting for Frank to amount to something."

Scott saw movements in the willows along the creek ahead of them, and he reached for his gun, suddenly wary as he remembered what had happened in town. Then he dropped his hand as a big man spurred his horse up the creek bank and came into the open. It was Delazon who swung his mount around and reined up, facing them. He sat his saddle there, blocking the road, his red face purple with the fury that gripped him.

Scott pulled up, motioning for Patsy to stop. He

said easily, "I figured you'd be up here."

Delazon licked meaty lips, fighting his temper. Then he exploded. "Of all the chuckle-headed idiots, you sure take the cake. If I'd known what you had between the ears for a brain, I'd have let you rot in that Nebraska jail."

Scott heard Patsy's sharp intake of breath. He leaned forward in the saddle, his voice low when he said, "I ain't one to brag about what I've got between the ears, but alongside you, I'm pretty bright. I don't reckon you've got a brain in your head. Maybe just the yolk of an egg." He paused, and added, "Scrambled."

Patsy giggled. "You're right, Mr. Travis, judging by the way he's been riding around trying to buy cattle and asking for delivery at Winnemucca."

"Never mind about that," Delazon snapped. "I told you to ride into town, Travis, size up the bank, and keep going. But what do you do? First thing you let Hibbard jump you on the street. Then you butt into the business between her"—he motioned toward Patsy—"and Bengogh. You bust Tally up, and you talk tough to Jimmy Kane. Now what's gonna happen when you ride back into town?"

"Dunno."

"Everybody will be looking at you. You're a marked man in Piute. You're no good to me now."

Scott lifted his reins. "Suits me."

"Wait." Delazon threw out a big hand. "I didn't mean that. You'll just have to cool your heels up here till folks forget you." He jabbed a finger at Patsy. "But fetching her up here tops everything. Why, damn it, why?"

"He picks up orphans and stray pups," Patsy said. "I'm the orphan. He's still looking for the pup."

"Get rid of her," Delazon shouted.

"How do you get rid of a redhead?" Scott asked.

"You found her," Delazon bawled. "It's your job to get rid of her."

"As I mentioned, you ain't no brainy jasper," Scott said. "After what you've been yapping about, getting me out of a Nebraska jug and all, don't seem it'd be smart to get rid of her."

"That's right," Patsy said complacently. "I know too much. You'll have to shoot me."

"I'd sure as hell like to." Delazon scratched his blob of a nose, eyes on Scott. "You've kept me waiting for two hours when I'm supposed to be at Runyan's Triangle R. I've got to keep this business up about buying cattle till we pull the job off."

"What job?" Patsy demanded. "If you think there's anything here that's worth—"

"Keep her with you, Travis," Delazon snapped. "Go on up the East Fork. The boys are camped just past where the road crosses the creek. I'll be along before dark." Cracking steel to his horse, he took off across the grass toward Runyan's Triangle R.

Scott looked at Patsy. "Well, you know."

"Not all of it," she said.

"I told you there was a couple of gents I had to meet. Won't be safe, coming with me. You'd better—"

"How was it you were going to get rid of me?" Patsy winked at him. "Quit worrying. I'm not afraid of any man living but Marvin Bengogh."

She was staring at Scott defiantly, her mouth a thin, stubborn line across her freckled face. No use, he thought. She'd follow him to hell and back. "All right," he muttered. "Let's mosey."

They climbed steadily for half an hour, the narrow road following the noisy creek. They were out of the valley and in the timber, the canyon walls rising on both sides of them. Here the big pines coolly shaded the bottom of the trough, and the air was dry and tangy with forest smells. Hoofs dropped silently into a thick mat of needles. Within a matter of minutes the valley was blotted out from sight below them and Scott Travis felt that he was in a new world.

The creek forked, the two canyons angling together. The road crossed the east branch and followed its north bank, and presently Scott saw the campfire. Two men were there. One was chopping wood, his ax making clear, ringing sounds against the pine, and the other was cutting steaks from a buck that hung from a limb.

"Stay here," Scott said, and rode toward the fire.

Both men heard him and wheeled, hands dipping toward gun butts. They stood motionless, staring at him as if shocked by absolute surprise; then one of them let out a squall. "Scott Travis, dang your mangy hide. Look at that, Ed. It's old Scott Travis."

"Thought they had you in the jug," the second man shouted.

Scott stepped down and shook hands, a sudden relief in him. He was as surprised as the men he had found. Delazon had never hinted that the men who would be here were Shorty Yates and Ed Bemis, Nebraska cowboys Scott had met in Ogallala at shipping-time—men he had painted the town with after they had been paid off.

"Well, sir," Scott said, "I was in the jug, all right, till a big gent named Delazon came along. I'm guessing I got out the same way you boys done."

"Heard about me?" Yates asked.

Scott nodded. "Horse-stealing, wasn't it?"

"That's what the damned granger sheriff claimed," Yates said bitterly, "but I didn't steal no horse. The case never got to a jury. I was rotting in that stinking jail when Delazon showed up talking about a fat little bank out here. After he got me augered into looking at that bank he showed up one night, shoved a gun into the jailer's belly, and out we walked."

"Same here," Bemis said glumly, "only I was in for rustling a milk cow from some sodbuster on the North Platte."

Scott nodded. "They had me in for murder, but it wasn't no such thing. The boss said we'd visit a fellow in a soddy on the Frenchman, which we done. We threw a little lead, and on the way home a posse jumped us. I had the bad luck to get my horse shot."

"So you're the one they nabbed," Bemis said.

"Yeah, I was the one. I thought I'd go loco, sitting in that jug and eating the swill they fetched me. Never would bring me to trial. I got the notion they didn't know how to get me off their hands."

Yates slapped his leg with his Stetson. "Reckon Delazon went around visiting jails and busting us out so he'd have him a crew of long riders. That's one way to do it."

"He said another man would be along, but he never said who it was," Bemis shook his head. "I kind o' wish I'd stayed put. Any idiot would know I wouldn't rustle a milk cow. I'd have had to milk her." He swore bitterly. "I was a damn fool. They was bound to let me out sooner or later."

"After I had a look at the Piute bank, I lost my hankering for Delazon's deal," Yates said morosely. "If there's five cents in that safe, I'll be surprised."

"Forget about me, Mr. Travis?" Patsy called.

She had ridden up and stopped ten feet from them. Scott swung around, grinning at her. "Sure did. Get down and meet a pair of long riders who likewise busted out of Nebraska jails. You've got to be careful, though. You can't trust 'em no farther'n you can throw your horse by the tail."

"Look who's talking," Yates jeered. "Ma'am,

this here ugly face would steal the drink right out of your glass if he caught you looking the other way."

Patsy stepped down, and Scott introduced them. Yates scratched his head, scowling. "What are you doing with her, Scott? Delazon didn't say nothing about no girl."

"I'm not his idea," Patsy said.

"She claims she'll help out on anything I figure on doing," Scott said. "She could hold the horses."

"But a girl—" Bemis began.

"A redheaded brat of a girl," Patsy cut in. "Sure I'll hold the horses. Shoot the sheriff. Anything. You see, I'm like a mustard plaster. Easy to stick on but awful hard to get rid of."

"That," Scott said gloomily, "is sure the truth."

"Mr. Travis is awfully kindhearted," Patsy said, smiling.

"Yeah, I collect orphans and stray pups, and I'm looking for the pup." Scott cuffed back his Stetson. "Maybe you boys can tell her this ain't no place for a girl."

"It ain't," Yates said.

"But I'm so useful," Patsy protested. "I'll cook your grub and fetch water and sweep out the bunkhouse." She wrinkled her nose at Yates. "And I'm an ornament."

Yates laughed. "Well, ma'am, you make it sound plumb convincing."

"She ain't got no place to go," Scott said. "I latched onto her in Piute—"

"He means I latched onto him." Patsy pinned her eyes on Yates's face, then looked at Bemis. "Sounds like Delazon fetched you boys out here to rob the Piute bank. That it?"

"That's it in a nutshell," Bemis agreed, "but we ain't bank robbers. We just made a deal with Delazon. That's all."

"Well, now, I've heard of all kinds of frauds, little

deals and big ones like Bengogh's working at, but this one is new." Patsy put her hands on her hips, smiling in the superior way of one who knows something they don't. "Gents, you might as well face it. You've been taken. There isn't enough money in that bank to pay you for your time."

Chapter 6: Delazon Talks

FOR A LONG MOMENT SCOTT STARED AT PATSY, A TIDE OF self-condemnation rising in him. He'd been taken, all right, taken by big, glib-talking Sam Delazon when he was rotting in jail and willing to reach for anything that promised escape. More than that, his outfit had left him high and dry, a fact which time finally forced him to recognize. Loyalty had always been a strong force in Scott Travis, but the weeks in that tiny cell had taught him a bitter lesson in human nature. Loyalty could be a one-sided thing.

He had expected to be broken out of the jail, or at least have his boss send a lawyer to see him, but he had been left strictly alone. Apparently the Easterner who owned the outfit didn't care what happened to a thirty-a-month cowhand who let himself get jailed when the crew made its first and only effort to intimidate a settler.

The jailer had finally told Scott his outfit was pulling out to avoid more trouble with the grangers. The herd had been gathered and was being pushed across the state line onto a new range in Colorado. Delazon had come to see him not long after that.

"They've crucified you," Delazon had said, "leaving you to these granger county officials who'll hang you just to make an example out of you.

You've got to get out of here if you want to save your hide."

They had met several years before when Delazon was rodding an outfit over on the Republican; then he'd dropped out of sight. Scott didn't know what had happened, and he didn't ask. It was enough for the fellow to slip him a gun and promise to leave a horse in the alley behind the jail.

Getting out had been easy—a little too easy, Scott was thinking now. If he hadn't been poisoned with hate for the jailer, the grangers, and his outfit that had left him stranded, he'd have been suspicious; but Delazon had posed as the only friend he had.

"Nobody ever gives a man anything," Delazon had said. "It ain't the meek who inherit the earth. It's them that gets out and grabs."

Delazon had talked a good deal about rich bankers who got fat picking the bones of little men, bankers who stayed inside the law but stole just the same—talk Scott had been in a mood to hear—and had painted a fine picture of the easy pickings in Piute, of other banks in Oregon and Washington, of getting an outfit together and a sure-fire method of himself going into a community to look it over before they cracked the bank. They'd be rich by the end of the year.

The horse had been there, all right. Scott had found a little money in a saddlebag and a map of Easter Valley. There had been no pursuit. Easy, all right. Scott had just pointed the gun at the jailer, locked him in his own cell, and walked out.

Now, after a long moment of silence, Scott looked at Yates and Bemis and guessed that the same thought had been in their minds that had been in his. Suddenly Yates burst out, "All right, so we've been taken if you know what you're talking about. But why did Delazon go to all the trouble to get us out here if the bank don't have any money in it?"

"Ask Delazon," the girl said. "He'll be along."

"I'll ask him, all right," Scott said, "and I'll bust his head open if he don't answer."

"What good will that do?" Bemis asked.

"We'll know the truth." Scott gave Bemis a wry grin. "You know, Ed, I feel better. Reckon I wasn't cut out for bank-robbing."

"Me, too," Yates said. "Well, I was about to fry some venison. Anybody hungry?"

"I'm always hungry."

Yates fried the steaks, and Bemis went back to woodchopping. Scott took care of the horses while Patsy brought water from the creek and made coffee. As they ate, Scott told Bemis and Yates what happened in town, omitting the part about stopping at Sally Runyan's house for a drink.

"Delazon said one thing that was true," he finished. "This Hibbard *hombre* ain't no great shucks of a sheriff."

Bemis got up and tossed a chunk of pine into the fire. He was a spare, knot-headed man, ageless as range men often are with a deep-lined, mahogany face that would look the same at fifty as it did at thirty-five. He was a good man in a fight. Scott remembered that from the last time they'd had a go at painting up Ogallala.

Yates was all right, too, prematurely bald-headed and wide of body with a pair of fists that worked like the hind hoofs of a mule. There might be something for the three of them here in the valley if Scott could make the other two see it. Bemis was the oldest and was a little sour about everything, but Yates was still filled with the optimism of youth. Now, rolling a smoke, it struck Scott that he would never find better partners, but Bemis would be hard to convince.

Bemis gave Patsy a long, studying stare. "Pardon me, ma'am," he said apologetically, "but I get the notion you've got something up your sleeve besides your purty arm."

"I have," she said frankly, "but it'll wait. I want to tell you about the bank. It belongs to an old man named Hank Nolan. He's got a young wife and three kids, and he's gambled on the people who were evicted. Loaned them enough to get them started."

"You don't want the bank robbed because he's your friend. That it?"

"That's it." She smiled disarmingly at Bemis. "Anybody in the valley will tell you the same thing I am. He's busted if the little ranchers don't get their beef to market this fall. There isn't much cash in the valley. One reason is that Bengogh doesn't use the bank. He writes drafts on the company's account in Boise, and those drafts circulate as money."

"Got any idea how much is in the bank safe?" Scott asked.

"Two or three thousand. It's just a guess, but I do know one thing. If you clean his safe out, you won't have much to split four ways."

"Delazon takes half," Yates said bitterly. "We split the other half."

Patsy laughed. "A fat split you'll have." She rose and, lifting the soot-blackened coffeepot from the fire, filled their tin cups. "If the bank was robbed, Nolan would probably be forced to sell the notes the bank holds to Bengogh. You can see what that would do."

"Does he need the north half of the valley?" Bemis asked.

"Just like he needs twelve toes. But remember that the company owns only half of the range it claims. As long as there are little outfits in the valley, Bengogh's bound to have trouble keeping them off the sections he don't own."

Scott tossed his cigarette stub into the fire. "You know, when I got out of the Broken Buttes this morning, it seemed to me this valley was the kind of place where I'd like to stay and own an outfit. Then when I was riding along the lake with Patsy, I got the same feeling again, like it was a country I'd dreamed about all my life and just then I recognized it."

Bemis snorted. "Gonna rustle a few of Bengogh's cows?"

"No. Looks to me like the little fry's short on guts. We might make a deal with them."

"Delazon's coming," Yates said.

The sun was almost down, and here in the timber the light was already thinning. Delazon's horse coming upstream made a vague shape among the shadows, and Scott breathed, "Get back, Patsy."

Delazon rode up to the fire, his voice booming out, "Hope that buck ain't et up yet."

"Get down," Scott said. "We've got talk to make."

Delazon dismounted, wary eyes on Scott's face. "What kind of talk?"

Scott saw that Patsy had stepped back from the fire, then he moved toward Delazon, his gaze meeting the big man's. "Patsy was just telling us that there ain't enough dinero in that Piute bank to make the job worth while."

Delazon began to swell up. "You taking her word over mine?"

"Figured I would," Scott said.

"All right." Delazon jerked a hand downstream. "Git out of camp. Take your redhead with you. Shorty and Ed can pull this off. Make a bigger split anyhow."

"I'm stringing with Scott," Yates said.

Delazon wheeled to face Bemis. "What about you?"

"Talk good, and I might listen," Bemis said.

"Then listen," Delazon shouted. "That bank is just like I said it was, the safe chuck full of gold and greenbacks. We made a deal, and I expect you boys to keep your word. I kept mine, and I didn't have no security when I used my money to stake you."

"The way you made it look, you knew we'd show up," Scott said. "You weren't taking no risks."

"Nothing's changed," Delazon said in a frantic voice. "If you'd kept out of trouble in town like I told you, this deal would have gone as smooth as silk. But no, you had to lose your head over a skirt. I've heard the talk about her and Bengogh. He ditched her, that's all. She was living down there by herself—"

Scott would have let him talk, thinking he'd work himself out on a limb, but Patsy's temper flared. She cried, "You're a liar," and, running to the fire, picked up the ax and threw it at Delazon.

Delazon yelled and ducked the ax. Straightening, he shouted, "You're to blame for this. I'll spank some sense into your little—"

"I reckon not," Scott said quietly. "You figured on me and Ed and Shorty taking the chances. If we go ahead with this deal, you're gonna ride with us."

Delazon swung to him, his face mottled. "I can't do that. They know me too well in this country. I took a big risk getting you boys out of jail. Now you're taking the word of a girl that ain't no better'n a—"

Scott hit him, a jolting right that knocked the big man on his heels and stopped his talk. He grabbed for his gun, cursing in a wild, flaying voice. Scott hit him again, knocking him flat on his back among the pine needles, the gun dropping from his hand.

Delazon got up and shook his head. He bawled,

"So you want it rough, do you, Travis?"

He rushed Scott, and suddenly all the doubts and suspicions that had been in Scott's mind as he made the long ride to Easter Valley became a certainty. He met Delazon's rush, cracking him with one fist and then the other, a wild unreasoning rage crowding him.

Scott made himself as hard to hit as a dust devil. Delazon kept pressing, throwing looping punches that never connected effectively, and all the time Scott punished him with slashing blows in the face. A solid right caught Delazon squarely on the chin, and he went down again. His hand fell on the handle of the ax Patsy had thrown at him; he gripped it and came to his feet, slobbering and bleeding and whimpering like an injured animal.

Patsy screamed, and Bemis yelled, "Drop that, you fool." And Yates bellowed, "I'll put a slug in you if you brain Scott."

But Delazon was out of his head. He came on with the ax gripped in both hands, his face a crimson mask. He lunged, making a wild sweep with the ax, and Scott ducked. Yates put a foot out and tripped Delazon, and when he went down Scott jumped on him.

He drove his knees hard against the small of Delazon's back. Breath gushed out of the big man; he tried to arch his back and could not find the strength. Scott drove a vicious down-swinging right against the base of his neck, a blow that would have broken the neck of a smaller man. Delazon went limp, and before Scott could hit him again Bemis had an arm around him and was pulling him off.

"He's done, Scott." Bemis shook him. "Can't you savvy that? You damned near killed him."

Sanity slowly replaced the crazy fury that had swept through Scott. He stood over Delazon, looking down at him and pushing Bemis away. He swung around and went down to the creek; he kneeled there and washed the blood and sweat from his face.

In the heat of the fight he had not realized Delazon had hit him, but now he found that his nose was bleeding and he had an ugly bruise on one cheek. He rose and went back to the others, so tired that he could barely force his legs to move, now that the reaction from his rage had set in.

"Are you hurt bad?" Patsy asked, putting her hands on his arms.

He shook her off. "No."

"Two fights in one day," the girl breathed. "Mister, you are a man."

"Wouldn't have been any man at all if he'd got his noggin split," Bemis said irritably.

Scott sat down with his back to a pine trunk. "I wasn't going to listen to him talk about Patsy that way."

"You gone on her?" Bemis demanded.

"No."

"How do you know what he said ain't true?"

Scott looked up at the lanky cowboy. "Ed, you want to pull them words back and let on like you never said 'em?"

Red-faced, Bemis said, "Yeah, I sure will. But, damn it, I don't see that you done any good jumping Delazon."

"Couldn't help it. Seems like all afternoon I've been pulling and hauling between going ahead with this crazy bank job or backing out. When I got to town it started working on me, and then Patsy said we were suckers. Reckon I lost my head, Delazon starting to talk about Patsy."

Yates had picked up the ax and Delazon's gun and moved them out of the man's reach. "I've been the same way about this bank job, Ed. So have you, although I ain't sure you know it."

"I know it, all right," Bemis muttered, "but we made a deal."

Delazon was sitting up now, feeling of his battered face in the dazed way of a man who wasn't quite sure what had happened. Then he remembered; he placed his hands against the ground and pushed himself back so that he could put his shoulders against the trunk of a pine.

"Travis," he said thickly, "you and me ain't done."

"I figure to be around here awhile," Scott said.

Yates moved toward Delazon and stopped a step from him, staring down at him. "Mister, you're gonna talk now, or what Scott done to you is nothing to what I'll do. Why did you fetch us out here?"

"To rob a bank."

"If there's twenty thousand in that tin can of a safe, it would be worth while. Can you guarantee there's that much?"

"Sure."

"All right," Yates said. "You're riding with us like Scott said a while ago. If you're lying, I'll put a window right between your eyes."

Delazon lowered his gaze. He felt of his bruised mouth and dropped his hand back to his side. "Okay, the deal's off; but I'm out five hundred apiece on you three. You owe me that."

"You'll get paid," Scott said. "Now why did you fetch us out here? I ain't heard you answer Shorty's question."

"I answered it," Delazon said sullenly.

Yates drew his gun and thumbed back the hammer. "You know something, Delazon? I sure am an impatient gent."

"You're working for Bengogh, aren't you?" Patsy asked.

Delazon struggled to his feet and put his shoulders against the tree. He stared at Yates's gun, color leaving his battered face except for the dark bruises that Scott's fists had given him. "All right," he said wearily. "Bengogh's giving the orders. Robbing the bank was his idea."

"Why?" Scott asked.

"He wants the notes Nolan holds. He's after all the valley, aiming to make this the biggest ranch the company owns. If he could get those notes, he'd have everybody moved out in a few months because the little fry can't raise any money unless they get a herd to Winnemucca this fall."

"What about Jay Runyan?" Patsy asked.

"He'd be forced out with the company surrounding him."

"So you high-tailed back to Nebraska where you used to live," Yates said, "knowing the grangers were running things. You nosed around till you located three of us who were crazy enough to do anything to get out of the jug. That it?"

"Yeah, that's it. Them county officials was glad to get rid of you when I promised 'em you'd leave the state."

"Get on your horse and make dust," Yates snapped, "before I lose my temper and blow your head off which I've got a hankering to do."

"Hold on, Shorty," Scott said. "We ain't bound by no agreements we made, things being like they are, but we owe him the money he spent on us."

"We can't raise fifteen hundred," Bemis said. "You're loco, Scott."

"Nolan will let you have it," Patsy said.

"What makes you think that?" Scott asked.

"Nolan respects men who pay their debts," she said. "I've got a notion about this business. I think Nolan will like it." She nodded at Delazon. "If you want your money, be at the bank tomorrow noon."

"I'll be there." Delazon lurched to his horse and,

gripping the horn, laboriously pulled himself into the saddle. "I've got some advice for you, Travis. You'd better light a shuck out of the country. Wick Tally and Jimmy Kane ain't real fond of you after what happened today."

He reined his horse around and rode away into the twilight.

Chapter 7: Rifles Speak At Night

BEMIS WALKED OVER TO THE FIRE AND THREW WOOD ON it. He stood motionless, scowling at the flames, a lanky, bow-legged man marked by his years in the saddle. There was this moment of silence, Patsy looking at Bemis, then Yates, and finally bringing her eyes to Scott, who was still sitting with his back to the pine.

"It strikes me you boys aren't afraid of Bengogh or anybody else," Patsy said. "That's what's wrong with the valley. I was thinking that as long as you owe Delazon—"

"We don't owe nothing to nobody," Bemis cut in. "Scott's just too damned honest for his own good."

"We made a promise which we ain't keeping," Scott said curtly. "That don't hurt my conscience none, Delazon aiming to cheat us like he was; but he did put out good money to get us here, and I aim to pay him."

"If you're fixing to stay here," Patsy said, "Hank Nolan is a good man to have on your side."

"I'm staying." Scott rose stiffly and walked to the fire. "I've done my share of nursing cows for thirty a month and beans. From now on they're gonna be my cows."

"Yeah, same here," Yates agreed. "This deal Delazon and Bengogh rigged up goes against my grain. I'd like to take 'em down a notch."

"You're both gabbing like a couple of magpies," Bemis said sourly. "We're all broke. The only way to get any cows of your own is to steal 'em, and I'd rather rob a bank."

"There's a way to do this without robbing Nolan's bank or stealing cows," Patsy said.

"How?" Bemis demanded.

"Fight Bengogh."

"Oh, hell!" Bemis rolled a smoke, staring sourly at the brown paper curling between his fingers. "You're working mighty hard to get us tangled up in a ruckus that ain't our fight."

"You're not above fighting for pay, are you?" Patsy asked.

"I've fought for pay more'n once." Bemis reached for a burning twig and fired his cigarette. "But I've never fought for a handful of IOU's and I won't now."

"Will you fight for cattle?" Patsy demanded.

Bemis stared at her, the cigarette dangling from the corner of his mouth, smoke making a shifting cloud before his face. "I might," he said. "How do you figure to work it?"

"Tomorrow we'll round up the little ranchers and have a meeting at Jay Runyan's place," the girl said. "They've got to get a drive through to Winnemucca this fall. You boys can take the job and let them pay you with young she stuff. Then you'll have your start."

"Drive across Bengogh's range, I suppose?"

"You'll have to."

Bemis gave Scott a sour grin. "Real smart, ain't she?"

"I'd like to take a shot at it," Scott said. "Ed, I done some thinking sitting in that damned jail. I'm twenty-five years old, and all I've ever done is take orders and make money for an Eastern dude who let me rot in the jug while he moved his herd out of the state. I made up my mind I'd never work for another man again."

Yates kicked a pine chunk back into the flames. "Same here. I reckon a man gets to living by habit. It's easier to work for somebody else than it is to start out for yourself; but that's what I'm gonna do."

"That thirty a month still looks good to me," Bemis said.

"All right, you ride out in the morning," Scott said. "Me 'n' Shorty will take a crack at this deal if Patsy thinks she can swing it." He stared at the fire. "A lot of things have happened since I hit Piute, and the first thing was the best. I stopped at a house and got a drink. A woman lived there, a single woman."

"Sally Runyan," Patsy cried. "Scott, I told you she was engaged to Frank Hibbard."

"She had a homey place," Scott went on as if he hadn't heard. "The kind of a house you'd like to stay in. Well, I'd been riding for days, and I was tired and thirsty and wishing to hell I was out of this bank business. Maybe I didn't know I was wishing it, but I do now." He looked directly at Bemis. "Ed, a man keeps going like he has been, or he lights somewhere and amounts to something. I aim to light."

"Well, I'll be damned," Yates murmured. "So it's a woman."

"A woman he saw once in his life," Bemis said. "You've been pasturing in some locoweed, boy."

"And all the time I thought it was this here redhead." Yates winked at Bemis. "Didn't you, Ed?"

"Sure did," Bemis answered with great gravity. "I was feeling plumb sorry for you, too, settling down with a fireball like her."

"Thank you, Mr. Bemis," Patsy said, "but I'm just the orphan. Maybe I'll get him to adopt me."

Scott was in no mood to be rawhided. He said more sharply than he intended to, "How about it, Ed? Shorty and me would like to have you for a partner."

Bemis flipped his cigarette stub into the fire. "I ain't going nowhere in the morning. Let's wait and see what happens when Red here gets her friends together."

Scott and Yates looked at each other, both satisfied that in the end Bemis would stay. "Well, I'm gonna roll in," Scott said. "I feel kind o' tired."

Later, with Bemis and Yates sleeping on the other side of the low-burning fire, Scott lay staring at the stars through the pine needles above him. There was no sound but the steady clatter of the creek with now and then the hooting of an owl or the haunting call of a coyote from a ridge.

Slowly the weariness and tension drained out of him and he relaxed, thinking back over the day and how it had changed his life. You go along through all the years, content to work for someone else, looking forward to a Saturday night in town. A game of poker. A dance. A drink with friends like Shorty Yates and Ed Bemis.

Satisfied. That was it, so satisfied that he hadn't thought much about cutting loose. But now it would never be the same again. He had not asked for the change that had come inside him; but it had come just the same, going back to that night when he had ridden with half a dozen cowboys to scare a settler out of his soddy.

In the past he had not been one to measure the

moral quality of any act—he had simply gone with the others because he had been given an order; but now he knew it had been wrong. His boss had been much like this Marvin Bengogh, taking orders from the owner who lived in the East. Probably he'd sent word to move the outfit and to hell with any of his men who made the mistake of getting caught and winding up in jail.

Well, that was behind him and he had no regrets about it. A man had to learn the hard way, and that was the way he himself had learned. What he wanted was here if he was tough enough to get it. In spite of himself, he thought of Sally Runyan. He wasn't sure that he wanted her, but he'd see her again and again until he was sure. If he did want her, Frank Hibbard wouldn't stand in his way.

He pictured her in his mind, her brown hair and dark eyes, her straight-backed, slender figure. He had seen many girls prettier than Sally Runyan. No, it wasn't her beauty that made him think of her the way he did. He had sensed a deep, inherent honesty in her, perhaps because she had boldly stated her dissatisfaction about conditions in the valley. For all she knew, he might have been someone Bengogh had hired. Still she had made no secret of her feelings.

He thought of his past again, and the discontent that had been growing in him became a painful ache. If he went on the way he had been living, he would become another Ed Bemis in ten years, a doubting man who had lost the ambition that must have been in him at one time, content to ride for his thirty a month and found. In time he would be like many old men he had known, swamping out saloons or waiting on bars if they were lucky, just hanging around to die. That wouldn't do for Scott Travis.

Suddenly he was aware that Patsy was sitting up.

He raised himself on an elbow, asking softly, "What is it?"

"I thought I heard something on the other side of the creek," she said. "Up there in the pines."

The fire had died down until it was a red hole in the pressing blackness. Patsy made a vague shape a few feet from him, her face a pale oval. He said, "You were dreaming."

"No, I've been awake. I couldn't go to sleep for some reason. Just worried, I guess."

"What about—your friends who maybe won't have the guts to buck Bengogh?"

"Partly. I was thinking about Delazon, too. We should have tied him to a tree or something."

"Why?"

"He'll hike out for the company ranch, and he'll tell Bengogh what happened."

"Well?"

"Don't you see? Bengogh will try another way to get at Nolan, and he'll rig up some way to get rid of you. He can't afford to have a man around who isn't afraid to fight. You've cut quite a swath today, Scott."

"We can't settle it now. You'd better start working on that sleep you haven't had."

"I guess so," she said, and lay back.

Then it came, a bullet raising a geyser of red coals from the fire and the crack of a rifle puncturing the mountain silence. Instinctively Scott lunged away from the fire, yelling, "Patsy." She had moved the same instant he had, diving for the shelter of the big pine Scott had leaned against after his fight with Delazon. Scott gripped her arm as more bullets peppered the spot where they had been lying, each report of the rifle as sharp as the snapping of a dry twig; then he pulled her behind the pine, the last bullet knocking bark from the tree trunk above them.

"You all right?" he asked.

"Sure," she whispered. "Just scared."

He put his arm around her and felt her tremble. He said, "You're all right now."

"Of course. I've just got the shakes."

"You were right about Delazon," he said. "We should have tied him to a tree, or knocked his head in."

Yates and Bemis had been sleeping on the creek side of the fire, and now Yates was cursing in a high, scared voice. Bemis shouted, "Shut up, you fool. You ain't hit, are you?"

"No," Yates said, and swore again. "But I jumped too damned far and fell into the creek."

Patsy giggled hysterically. "Cold night for a bath," she said, her teeth chattering.

"Stay down," Scott called. "He'll open up again soon as he gets his rifle loaded."

"You're damned right we're staying here," Bemis said. "I couldn't budge if I wanted to. Shorty's shoving me into the bank."

"Stay here, Patsy," Scott said. "Don't move."

"I couldn't," she whispered. "I couldn't move an inch."

The rifleman opened up again, spraying the area around the fire with lead. Scott, hugging the pine trunk, moved his head enough to look past it at the south slope of the canyon and saw the ribbonlike tongues of powder flame. He drew his head back. The man wasn't far away, but there was no telling what sort of shelter he had. Probably he was crouched behind a boulder.

Again the firing died, and Bemis called, "Scott, are you up to something?"

Scott didn't answer. He had a little time now before Delazon could reload. He was certain it was Delazon—that, pretending to ride away, he had circled back on the other side of the creek. A braver man would have sneaked in close, and he might have got all of them before they found cover.

Scott's Colt was in holster, the gun belt beside his saddle where he had been lying. The fire was still a faint rosy glow, and Delazon was probably close enough to catch a blur of movement in that thin light. It was possible he had held back a shell for such an opportunity. Scott decided against trying for his six-gun. Instead he slipped away from the pine, remembering where he had left his Winchester but not sure he could find it in the darkness.

Bemis called again. "Scott, what are you doing?"

Patsy said, "He's gone. He's not going to answer you."

"That knucklehead," Bemis shouted angrily. "That crazy knucklehead."

Scott moved through the trees to where the horses had been staked. He had leaned his Winchester against a small pine, but in this absolute darkness with the starlight blanketed by the timber, one tree was like another, and he had to move slowly, feeling around each trunk with his hands. Time ribboned out into what seemed an eternity before he found the Winchester, and then in his haste he knocked it over and had to get down on his knees and fumble in the thick mat of needles before he found it again.

As he straightened up, Delazon started in again just as he had before, throwing lead around the fire. Scott was a safe distance from it; he levered a shell into the chamber and standing beside the tree where he had left his Winchester, he took a moment to spot the rifle flashes. He let go then, firing as rapidly as he could at the spot where the man must be. His first shot silenced the other rifle.

When the Winchester was empty Scott lowered

it, listening, and a moment later heard what he had been certain he would, the receding drum of hoofs. There was probably a cattle trail on the crest of the ridge. He went back to the fire. "You boys can crawl out now. Our friend's gone."

Yates poked his head up over the bank. "Sure?"

"If your teeth wasn't rattling so you couldn't hear, you'd know he was gone."

"I ain't scared." Yates came toward Scott. "I ain't scared for a minute, but, damn it, that creek water's cold."

Bemis crawled over the bank and stood up. "Scott, you ain't gonna live long enough to make that drive across Bengogh's range."

"I dunno 'bout that," Scott said. "I wasn't taking any chances." He kicked the coals toward the creek, and there was only the dying glow of a few sparks. "I figured he'd take off when some lead started going the other way. Delazon's a little short on guts."

"Don't take much guts to dry-gulch a man," Bemis said. "Now you've got both Delazon and that Wick Tally gunning for you."

"I ain't worried," Scott said. "Not much. Patsy, where are you?"

"Right where you left me," she answered. "I'll be down there with you as soon as my knees will hold me."

Yates laughed. "Don't hurry. You've got all night. The rest of you can go to sleep again. I've got to keep moving or I'll freeze to death. Sure wish I could build the fire up."

"Probably be safe enough," Scott said. "I'm guessing Delazon will light out for the company ranch to see Bengogh."

"No fire," Bemis said sharply. "We ain't taking no more chances. Hell, we should have thought of that polecat coming back."

"Wake me up in a couple of hours and I'll stand guard," Scott said.

They moved their saddles and blankets into the timber away from the creek, but still Scott found sleep elusive. He was thinking now about what Delazon had said, that Kane and Tally would not forget what had happened in town. Pride was a compelling motive in men like that, and their pride had been injured so that nothing but his own death could heal the wound.

Still, it was not really Wick and Kane that worried Scott. Nor Delazon. The sly and scheming Bengogh was the one to look out for. He would sense danger in Scott's presence in the valley; he would act suddenly and violently in a manner that neither Scott nor Patsy could foresee.

Chapter 8: The Fox

OF MARVIN BENGOGH'S MANY TALENTS, THE ONE WHICH had most consistently proved valuable to him in this country which he hated was his ability to mask his feelings behind an inscrutable countenance. Before he met Alec Schmidt's young wife Ellen, he had been a gambler and a good one. Now he was thankful for the hours he had spent at a poker table. He could smile in a man's face while he killed him, letting no one guess that fear that raveled down his spine and lay deep in his belly like a piece of ice that refused to melt.

The fear had been there when he had watched Patsy Clark throw down on him with her rifle. He had never been closer to death, yet he felt no obligation to the stranger who saved his life. As soon as he stepped back into the saloon, he took a quick drink, thankful for the relaxation that the whisky brought to him.

He watched with small concern the fight between Wick Tally and the stranger. When they brought Tally's limp body into the saloon and sloshed water on him, he smiled with detached amusement as the man came to and lashed out blindly with his fists. A fat cowboy who had helped carry him in jumped back, saying testily, "You're a little late, Wick. He's gone."

Tally sat up, feeling of his face and spitting blood from a bruised mouth. He said thickly, "Where'd that *hombre* find the clubs he hit me with?"

Jimmy Kane snorted his derision. "He didn't need no club, Wick. Just his fists, and you're supposed to be such a hell of a fighting man."

Tally got to his feet and propped himself against the bar. He sleeved water from his face and gingerly felt of his battered mouth. He looked at Bengogh. "I reckon we go after him, don't we, boss?"

"No," Bengogh shrugged. "He's just a drifter. Probably be out of the country by night."

"Rode off with the Clark girl," the fat buckaroo said.

"That doesn't make any difference. Nothing here to hold him. We've got bigger fish to fry than a fiddle-foot like that."

"I don't cotton to the notion of letting him go," Jimmy Kane said. "We've put in a lot of time making sheep out of these settlers. Let some tough *hombre* like that drift in, and the first thing you know the sheep will be turning into wolves."

Bengogh laughed easily. "Jimmy, I'll tell you something about people. You can turn men into sheep, but you can't make sheep into wolves."

"You had a chance at him, Jimmy," the fat buckaroo said.

Kane wheeled on the fat one. "You making out I was afraid of him, Chubby?"

"Hell, no!" The buckaroo backed away. "You've got enough fighting to do without kicking up a fracas with me."

"That's right," Bengogh said sharply. "You know your business, Jimmy, so I'm not asking any questions; but if he does hang around you'll have another opportunity. If he doesn't no harm's been done." He nodded at Tally. "I've some business in the bank. We'll be riding in about half an hour."

Bengogh left the saloon, hiding his sour thoughts behind his expressionless face. He hated anything that smelled of defeat; he had hired Wick Tally and Jimmy Kane to prevent this very thing. So far they had served their purpose, but today they had failed.

There was more danger in what Jimmy Kane had said about this stranger turning sheep into wolves than Bengogh cared to admit. No one understood better than he that men are creatures of habit, and either defeat or victory can become a habit.

And there was Patsy Clark. The fellow was with her, and she was someone to be afraid of. Bengogh reluctantly admitted to himself that the death of Patsy's father had done more harm than good; and now he realized that Patsy might be able to make real trouble. He had hoped she would take his offer of a job and be satisfied. He should have known better, but the truth was he had not given the girl much thought.

Bengogh stopped at the post office for his mail. Thumbing quickly through the envelopes, he found one he had been expecting for days, addressed in the beautiful, elaborate handwriting with which he was familiar.

Slipping the other envelopes into his coat pocket to read when he got back to the ranch, he opened the one from Ellen Schmidt. It was dated three days ago, and he mentally cursed the slowness of the mail. He might be short of time, and everything depended on Alec Schmidt's approving of what he found when he reached Easter Valley.

He scanned the letter, frowning when he realized that Ellen was saying she and her husband would reach the valley late Friday afternoon—and today was Friday. He swore softly. He should have anticipated this, for it was like Alec to be very indefinite about when he would make his inspection, and then arrive suddenly.

Ellen closed with a formal *Yours truly*. Probably Alec had read and approved that part of the letter; but before sealing it she had added a postscript: *It's been so long, darling, so long. We must arrange it so Alec will bring you back to San Francisco this fall. I simply cannot live this way, seeing you just once in two years.*

Bengogh dropped the letter into his pocket, filled with a sense of well-being. The first time he had seen Ellen, he had sensed she would not be satisfied to live as the wife of an old man. She was too young, too vital. She was clever, and old Alec was completely in love with her—two facts which were responsible for Bengogh's having his chance here in Easter Valley.

He did not once doubt Ellen's ability to persuade the old man that he was wasting a good man on this remote fringe of his empire. By fall he would be back in San Francisco, back in civilization and away from the wilderness, and he would begin to live again. And he would see Ellen as often as he wanted to. It would work out all right, he told himself as he left the post office, for there was little on the company ranch that Alec could find wrong.

As he turned toward the bank a twinge of worry cut in on his satisfaction. Ellen had been foolish to add that postscript. Alec might have read it. If he suspected anything he might have steamed the envelope open without her knowing; and then the dreams and plans which they had nurtured so carefully would be destroyed. He would have to tell her to be more careful. They could not afford to gamble now.

Hank Nolan was alone in the bank. Bengogh said pleasantly, "How are you, Hank?"

Nolan stepped to the gate at the end of the counter, frowning as if he sensed the reason for the visit. He said, "Howdy, Mr. Bengogh. It's a miracle that you're alive."

"It is at that." Bengogh laughed easily. "Patsy was riled, wasn't she?"

"Nothing to laugh about," the banker said. "You had one foot inside the pearly gate. You can't blame Patsy, either."

"You can hardly blame me, if you want to talk about blame. I leaned over backward trying to be fair with her, and she tries to kill me. That's gratitude for you, Hank."

"You don't understand these people, Mr. Bengogh," Nolan said wearily. "Regardless of your company's legal rights, the fact remains that Patsy and her neighbors were here several years before your company bought the wagon-road grant. When they settled on the lake they had no way of knowing the grant extended this far."

"They could have gone to the land office."

"It's a long trip to Lakeview, and they didn't think it was necessary. In this country settlers have always considered squatters' rights strong enough to hold their homes."

Bengogh lifted a cigar from his coat pocket and bit off the end, not liking this turn in the conversation. He secretly admired Hank Nolan, a queer-

looking little man—not even as tall as himself—
who wore chin whiskers and shaved the rest of his
face clean. Now he stood at the end of the counter,
stroking his beard and letting Bengogh feel his
hostility.

"I didn't come in to talk about Patsy." Bengogh
fired his cigar. "My orders are to clear company
range of settlers. Mr. Schmidt assumed, when he
bought the grant, that we would control the alternate sections. In time we shall secure title to them."

"Until then these sections are open to settle-
ment," Nolan said doggedly. "By the use of force
you have driven people from their homes into the
northern half of the valley."

"Not force, Hank," Bengogh said.

"By the threat of force, then."

"I'm the manager of just one of thirty ranches
that the company owns," Bengogh said. "I didn't
come in to discuss Mr. Schmidt's policy. I just want
to know if you have reconsidered selling the notes
you hold."

"No." Nolan's sallow, deeply lined cheeks
turned red. "I will not sell my friends out. I thought
I made that clear."

"You wouldn't be selling them out," Bengogh
said persuasively. "I couldn't collect those notes
until their due date, and by that time you'll have to
collect them yourself to meet your own obligations."

"Why do you want them?"

"Two reasons. I hope to keep you solvent because
we need a bank in the valley. The second reason is a
matter of self-preservation. It's easier to control all
the valley than half of it. This is big cattle country,
Hank. You know that."

"No, I don't know that," Nolan said with asperi-
ty. "Our nation's strength lies in the small farmers

and ranchers and businessmen, not in an octopus which reaches from the Mexican border to Easter Valley. I'll keep those notes to prevent you from doing the very thing you want to do."

There was one hole in the little banker's armor, and now Bengogh drove a knife into that hole. "Hank, let's look at this realistically. You're an old man, too old to start over and too old to work for anybody else. You have a young wife and three children who will be dependent on you for a long time. Are you considering them?"

Nolan bowed his head, fighting for self-control, and it was a moment before he could say, "You're a smart man, Mr. Bengogh, a smart, sly man."

"I'm just trying to look ahead for you as well as myself."

"Now you're a hypocrite." Tears ran down the old man's cheeks. "A fork-tongued hypocrite. Go to hell!"

With any other man Bengogh would have been furious; but not with Hank Nolan. The old banker possessed a dogged courage that Bengogh was very conscious he lacked; so he must fake it, depending on men like Jimmy Kane and Wick Tally to put teeth into his scheming.

"Let me know when you change your mind," he said, and walked out.

Dissatisfaction was working in Bengogh again. Hank Nolan was a hard man to fight, but he'd be brought around in a day or two. Still, it was disappointing. This would have been the easier and safer way.

He went into the saloon, calling, "Time to ride," and motioned to the fat buckaroo. When the man came up to him he said, "Chubby, I just had word that Mr. and Mrs. Schmidt will be here tonight. You hike out and meet them, and take them directly to the ranch. You can save them several hours of travel." He smiled in his easy way. "They will appreciate it."

"Sure, I'll fetch 'em in," Chubby said, and wheeled out of the saloon.

Later, riding at the head of his crew, Bengogh lost his sourness and worry as pride ran through him. Wick Tally rode on his right, a tall man who sat his saddle in the way of one who belonged there. Jimmy Kane was behind him, glancing around warily as one does who constantly expects danger. The others were all right in their way, many of them vaqueros who had come north with the company herd. Nowhere could a man find better hands with cattle.

Bengogh had been born and raised on a Texas ranch—the one fact which enabled Ellen to persuade her husband that he should have a chance with the Easter Valley ranch. In the two years he had been here he had demonstrated that he knew the cattle business; and he was not above giving a hand at spring and fall roundup when help was short.

He never doubted the loyalty of his men. All but Kane and Tally had worked for the company on its California or Nevada ranches, and, as far as Easter Valley was concerned, Marvin Bengogh was the company. He glanced speculatively at Wick's wind-burned face. He was different. Kane, too. With them loyalty was a commodity which could be bought, and he would hold that loyalty as long as he was capable of paying for it.

When they were directly east of Patsy's cabin, Bengogh hipped around in his saddle. "Jimmy, take Lane and Sandoval and ride over to the Clark place. If Patsy's still there, give her a nudge."

Kane grinned and licked his lips. It was a chore he relished. "Sure hope that tough drifter's there."

"No trouble," Bengogh said sharply. "This isn't the time for it. I'm expecting the Schmidts tonight."

"Sure, no trouble," Kane agreed, and swung his horse toward the Clark cabin, the grin still clinging to the corners of his mouth.

Wick was silent for several minutes. He was not a talkative man, and now his bruised mouth made talking difficult, but he said at last, "That was a mistake, boss. Jimmy don't look for trouble. He makes it."

Bengogh never liked to be told he had made a mistake. He said curtly, "It'll be all right," and let it drop.

The road bent away from the lake. Bengogh glanced toward it, studying the vast sweep of the tule marsh. Good land if it was drained and the tules cleaned out. If Ellen's plan failed and he was forced to remain here another year, that would be his next job; it was the sort of job Alec liked, because it increased the value of his holdings. If on the other hand Ellen succeeded, he would mention it to Alec so the old man would know he was looking ahead, planning for the company's future.

It was still early in the afternoon when they reached the two-story, frame ranch house, which stood tall and white in the glaring sunlight like a fine monument. In a way it was exactly that, a monument to Bengogh's two years in the valley. When he had come, there had been nothing but the grass belly-high on a horse that had been wasted for centuries.

Bengogh stepped down, handing his reins to a vaquero, eyes sweeping the great barn and sheds and stockade corrals. There were other stockade corrals in the valley; but these were the strongest, made of willows interlaced between juniper posts and held in position by rawhide thongs. He had taken great care with them. Neat. Clean. Orderly. The way Alec liked his ranches. He, Marvin Bengogh, had done this in two years. He was certain the old man would give him the credit he deserved.

He walked into the house and went on back to the kitchen. He said to the Chinese cook, "The Schmidts will be here tonight. Pay attention to your supper, Chang."

Chang bobbed his head and smiled blandly. "I cook extra good."

Bengogh turned and went into his office. He stayed at his desk all afternoon, putting everything down in neat rows of figures that Alec would want to examine. That was Alec. Economy, accuracy, order; those were the rules of his life, and they at least partially accounted for his success.

Near evening Bengogh was finished. He had known that Alec would be here sometime during the summer, and had not let his work pile up on him. He opened the safe and took out all but one of the sacks of money. Carrying them upstairs, he hid them under his mattress. It was a precaution against the possibility that Ellen's plans would fail. He had drawn more drafts against the company accounts in a Boise bank than Alec would approve of, but it would be all right.

In the short time Alec would be here he could not discover that any cash was missing. It was well covered. Or, if it did come out, he could say he had accumulated it to buy out the little ranchers the instant they saw they were going under. At least he had enough to start somewhere else if his plans with Ellen did not work out. She would go with him. Perhaps to The Dalles. He had heard it was a good town for a man who possessed both cash and clever fingers.

Dusk had flowed across the valley when Bengogh heard the buggy. He stepped out on the porch, calling, "It's fine to see you again, Alec," and crossed the yard.

Chubby dismounted, saying, "Mr. Schmidt's tapeworm is hollering, boss."

"Supper's ready," Bengogh said, and held out his hand to Schmidt, who had laboriously got down from the buggy.

"Good," Schmidt said, giving Chubby the lines. "I am hungry."

He was a big, ponderous man who refused to dress like a stockman and looked like a storekeeper in any average Western town. His breath came with an effort as he shook hands with Bengogh, who noticed at once that the old man had failed a great deal in the last two years.

Bengogh turned to help Ellen from the buggy. She was a tall, supple woman with more color than he had ever seen in anyone as blond as she was. To him she was the most beautiful woman in the world; and he had often let himself dream of their life in San Francisco after Schmidt was dead and he and she were married. More than anything else, that dream had supported him through the two lonely years in Easter Valley.

"Thank you, Marvin." Ellen gave his hand a squeeze. "I do hope Chang has a good meal. Alec has been hungry for hours."

The men came streaming across the yard—all but Jimmy Kane and Wick Tally, who had never worked for Schmidt and did not know him. The old man shook hands with all of them, asking about the health of each. The vaqueros bowed and grinned, saying, "Bueno, señor—the climate, she is fine," or "You should see the calves, señor—they were never so big in California."

After the greetings Bengogh led the Schmidts into the house. Ellen took off her linen duster and handed it to him, and he hung it on the hall rack, saying, "Your room is at the head of the stairs, first door to your right. I'll bring your luggage up."

Her blue eyes touched his face briefly. She murmured, "I'll find it," and smiled.

They ate a few minutes later, Schmidt shaking the cook's hand as if he were a close personal friend. The old man had a warm, personal touch that bound a thousand riders, managers, cooks, and laborers to him, all the way from the Mexican line to Easter Valley. When he died the company would lose something no other man could give it.

Bengogh was as surprised as the Schmidts when the cook brought a heaping platter of fried chicken to the table, bowing in the manner of a serf serving his lord.

"Chicken!" Schmidt exclaimed. "What do you know about that? I didn't suppose there was a chicken in twenty miles of here."

"Boys blought 'em," Chang said proudly. "Chang cook 'em."

"It's a wonderful treat," Ellen said.

A vague uneasiness crept over Bengogh. This was Jimmy Kane's doings. He had stolen Patsy Clark's chickens, and that meant trouble, Patsy being the girl she was. Wick Tally had been right; he shouldn't have sent Kane to the Clark cabin.

After supper Ellen went upstairs, saying she was tired, and Bengogh led Schmidt to the office. For two hours they went over the books, the old man nodding occasionally or grunting approval. When they were done Bengogh said, "A fine calf crop, Alec. It's like I've written to you. We could run twice or three times as many cows as we're running now."

"Are the settlers off the grant?" Schmidt asked.

"All of them."

"Any trouble?"

"No. I would even go as far as to say that by the end of the year they'll be out of the valley. This is big cow country, Alec, your kind of cow country." Bengogh leaned forward. "And something else. Next year I plan to drain the marsh around the lake, providing you're willing to hire men to do it. It would make the best hay land in the world and more than repay the cost of draining it."

Schmidt leaned back in the swivel chair and filled his pipe, smiling contentedly. "I'm pleased with what you've done, Marvin. I'll admit I was skeptical at first, but Ellen kept ding-donging at me that you were the best man I had. Now I'm considering returning you to the home office at the end of the year as general superintendent."

Bengogh was properly surprised. "I can't express my—"

"Don't try." Schmidt pulled hard on his pipe. "Now there is one thing. I expect to send a man north in the fall to take this job, and I want you to remain with him for at least three months. Work with him. Tell him all your plans. Get him started."

"I'll be glad to do that," Bengogh said, masking his surprise and dissatisfaction. He would have to stay here another five or six months.

"I'll be honest in saying I will send a man in whom I have complete confidence. Your promotion will depend on a vote of my board of directors, and that in turn will be determined by the word of the man who takes your place."

Again Bengogh was glad for the years of poker-playing that had taught him to hide all feeling behind an expressionless face. Now bitterness washed through him like a corrosive acid. Alec's board of directors always did as he said, so the old man was indirectly saying that he was still on probation.

"I'll do my best to satisfy your man," Bengogh said.

Schmidt rose. "And I'm sure you will. When I bought the wagon-road grant, I expected to control the entire valley. Naturally I'm looking for results, and I will not examine your methods too closely unless you provoke a range war which would put us in a bad light." He moved toward the door and then turned back. "Tomorrow I'll rest, and the next day we'll take a look at those calves you've been talking about. Then Ellen and I will start back. I've been out of touch with things too long already."

He left the room filled with the sickening stench of his pipe, and climbed the stairs. Bengogh swore, anger having its way. Fear was in him, too. He felt sweat break through his skin. He raised his hand and wiped it across his face.

It was going to be all right, he told himself. It had to be. The old man would probably not live another year. But it wasn't settled. Three months with a man Alec trusted, perhaps a man who disliked Bengogh. There were half a dozen such men who had been with the company for years.

Schmidt had just said he would not stand for a range war. As for violence, he had always said it was too expensive for the side that owned anything, while the little fellows didn't have anything to lose but their lives. He had found ways to destroy his enemies politely and neatly and had never, as far as Bengogh knew, hired men like Wick Tally and Jimmy Kane.

Bengogh blew out the lamp and went to his room. There he sat smoking, with the door open. Ellen would come as soon as Alec was asleep; but his mind was not on her. He thought of his enemies, particularly of two women he feared more than any man in the valley—Patsy Clark, who would not be satisfied until he was destroyed, and Sally Runyan, who made no secret of her hatred and might be able to persuade her brother to fight. And there was the tough stranger who had left town with Patsy.

Then Ellen slipped through the door and closed it softly, her eyes bright with the pleasure of seeing him. She stood there a moment, a tall, smiling woman with a talent for satisfying the passion that was in a man, a woman he could be proud of anywhere and any time.

"It's fixed, Marvin," she breathed. "Everything we wanted."

He rose and put down his cigar. He held out his arms, and she came to him; she kissed him, her hungry arms clutching him, and she let him feel the greedy desire that was in her.

She drew her mouth back, a hand caressing his cheek. "I love you, Marvin. I don't know why I love you so much, but I do. You're everything I want."

"I'll always try to be," he said, making his voice humble. "But Alec's sending—"

"Don't be silly. I'll pick the right man to send." She pulled him down on the bed and lay beside him. "We're together now. Let's be satisfied with what we have."

He could not sleep after she had gone. He could not remove the thought from his mind that these two years might have been wasted, two raw, bitter years without a woman, without any of the luxuries and comforts that he valued. He had never made a bigger gamble in his life. Well, he had to win. He'd make damned sure he won.

Dawn was a gray promise in the east when he heard the front door open. Irritated, he rose and pulled on his pants, realizing that something had gone wrong. Of all nights, it had to be this night.

Alec would be here only a day or two. To hell with trouble after he was gone, but now it had to be averted.

He felt his way down the stairs, then heard Wick Tally ask softly, "That you, boss?"

"Sure it's me! Light a lamp before I break my neck."

A match flared, and Tally held it to a lamp. As he slipped the chimney into place, the light showed Jimmy Kane behind him, and Delazon in the doorway, his face as battered as Tally's.

"Damn you," Bengogh burst out. "I told you never to come here."

"Had to," Delazon muttered. "The deal's off."

"Keep your voice down, boss," Tally murmured. "You've got big company."

Bengogh crossed the room to stand before Delazon, a sense of impending disaster nagging him. "All right, speak your piece."

Delazon told what had happened, his eyes on the floor. He said, "I circled back and took some shots at 'em from the other side of the creek. I don't reckon I hit 'em, but thought I might scare 'em into leaving."

"With that Clark bitch with 'em?" Bengogh snarled. "All you did was to make them mad, you clobber-headed fool."

Delazon lifted defiant eyes. "Don't call me that. I couldn't help it. I'm lucky to be alive."

"Too damned bad you are." Bengogh began to pace the floor, his quick mind gripping this turn. Then he wheeled back to Delazon. "You say this Travis fellow will be in town at noon?" When Delazon nodded he turned to Kane. "Jimmy, you know how to deal with tough drifters. Wick, you'd better be on hand in case anything goes wrong."

Kane grinned. "Nothing will go wrong, boss. I'll take care of him all right."

"The bank—" Delazon began.

"It'll wait. This chore comes first. Now get the hell out of here."

Bengogh went back to his room and lay down, but he still could not sleep. He began to sweat, the weakness of fear working in him as he remembered the way Travis had handled himself in town.

He cursed the day he had met Delazon; he cursed the deal he had made, and he cursed Delazon. An outburst of violence in the valley would ruin everything. Smooth! That was Alec Schmidt. Honey and oil were his weapons, not guns.

Slowly confidence returned to him, and the fear fled. He had picked Jimmy Kane carefully because of his gun speed and the cold-blooded pleasure he gained from killing a man. Travis could do no harm after he was dead.

Death was the one final solution to a great many things. Then a new thought occurred to Bengogh. Suppose Alec was to die now? He carefully considered it, savoring the possibilities. Nothing could keep Ellen from him then—nothing.

He got up and walked to the window. He stood there, staring out across the grass, the dawn light steadily deepening. This must be done with great care, for it was the one thing Ellen would not stand for. In a strange, detached way, she was fond of Alec. He lighted a cigar and began to pace the floor, considering ways and means while the sun came up and flooded the valley with scarlet light.

Chapter 9: Deal With Runyan

SCOTT WOKE AT DAWN TO FIND THAT YATES HAD A FIRE going. Patsy had gone to the creek to fill the coffeepot. He rubbed his eyes and sat up, feeling thoroughly tired and beaten. He said grumpily, "Might as well be on roundup."

Patsy came back up the slope, the dripping coffeepot in her hand. "It is roundup," she said. "Get on your feet. Time to rise and shine."

"Still full of vinegar." Yates winked at him. "Dunno how she does it when the sun ain't even up." He prodded Bemis awake. "Boss says it's time to rise and shine."

"I'll rise but danged if I'll shine," Bemis grunted. "Trouble and a redheaded woman sure come twins."

"We haven't had any trouble yet," Patsy said cheerfully. "I thought we'd get an early start and go meet it."

The sun was up by the time they left camp, Patsy leading. The winy air was cool and clear, and when they rode out of the canyon to follow a ridge that paralleled the mountains the valley spilled out below them, a rich green floor under the bright sun.

Reining up, Patsy motioned southward. "Room for all of us out there. Bengogh doesn't think so, but it's the way Uncle Sam meant for it to be."

They stopped, Bemis saying a little grudgingly, "Looks good, for a fact."

From this distance the lake seemed very small, a blue jewel surrounded by the dark green of the tule marsh, and all around it was the grass, sweeping out to fade into the dull gray of sage and rabbit brush.

The pile of ashes that had been Patsy's cabin would be nothing more than a grim, forbidding spot in the grass, a little island of death in a green sea of life. Scott Travis, who had prided himself on his toughness, discovered that he wasn't tough at all when he thought of the graves out there, of Patsy's father who had wanted to fight, of her mother who had not even wanted to live after Pat Clark had been killed.

Courage and love and hope and faith, all had been there, the invisible structure upon which the throbbing vitality of life in a new country must depend. Without it, no one survived; because of it, Pat Clark had died. Now there remained just the ashes, a stockade corral, a shed, and two graves. And the chickens, penned up to keep the coyotes from them.

Scott glanced at Patsy's taut face, sensing the poignant thoughts that were crowding through her mind, and violence began to throb in him like a pulse. He said in a low tone, "God damn Bengogh, God damn him."

Without a word, Patsy turned her horse and rode eastward, her head bowed. The men followed, Bemis and Yates glancing at Scott and not fully understanding. They followed the fringe of timber, the slope dropping away to their right until it became the nearly level floor of the valley.

A few minutes later Patsy looked back, her face composed. "I thought we'd swing around by George Vance's place. His oldest boys are big enough to ride."

Within the hour they reached Vance's ranch, a small cabin, a log barn, and a pole corral, evidence of newness still marking the place. As Patsy had said, he had picked a poor spot for a ranch with the wall of timber crowding the buildings. The slope to the south, covered by rabbit brush, held little grass, and nowhere was there the slightest hint of a hay field. Scott, reining up, wondered why Vance had come here.

A black-and-white dog of uncertain ancestry came yapping toward them, and was not silent until Patsy said sharply, "Shut up, Nip." He sat down and yawned pleasantly, his tail thumping the dust.

The cabin door was flung open, and a man stepped into the sunshine, his cheeks cherry-bright. His voice sailed out. "It's a good morning when I see you, Patsy. Light and eat. I fetched in an antelope yesterday."

He was comical, with a thin face and a bristling yellow mustache that gave him the appearance of a vicious demon who had just stepped from the pages of some ancient fairy tale; but there was nothing vicious about George Vance. Good nature seemed to ooze from him as he crossed the yard.

"George, I want you to meet three fighting men," Patsy said, and introduced them.

Vance shook hands all around, saying, "Glad to know you, boys. Fighting men are what this range needs, providing they're on Patsy's side." He swung around, bawling, "Missus, cut up the rest of the antelope. We've got company."

"We can't stay, George," Patsy said. "Got a lot of riding to do today. We're fixing to stir up some trouble for a gent named Marvin Bengogh."

Vance gave her a cocky grin. "That's something I've been waiting to hear for a long time."

A big woman in a faded-calico dress came out of the cabin, and a herd of children poured after her, all but the two older boys taking refuge behind her ample skirt. She had, Scott thought, the expressionless face of all pioneer women. Probably she had never known anything but disappointment and sorrow and hardship, and stoically faced a future that would hold the same. He tried to count the children and gave it up, wondering how she managed to keep such a brood in one small cabin.

"Clara," Patsy said, "I want you to meet three friends of mine who like this valley well enough to stay and fight for a piece of it."

"That'll suit George." Mrs. Vance slapped a boy who was yanking a girl's pigtails. "He's been hankering for a fight ever since we left the lake." She cracked a girl across the head who was trying to steal a biscuit from a toddler. "Born to die young, George was."

She crossed to them and shook hands, the children huddled in front of the cabin, staring with bright, half-frightened eyes, their elfin faces pinched by hunger. Probably they hadn't enough to eat since they left the lake; but neither George Vance nor his wife Clara showed the slightest hint of worry or fear. They had antelope today, Scott thought, so they had no concern about tomorrow.

"George, we want you to send your oldest boys to the neighbors today," Patsy said. "Tell everybody to meet at the Triangle R tonight. We're going to have a powwow and make big medicine."

Vance wheeled to the boys who were watching from the corner of the cabin. "Heard her, didn't you?"

As they scurried toward the corral, Patsy said, "I burned my cabin yesterday, but the chickens are penned up. You go get them, George. Pay me when you can."

"Sure, I'll go get 'em, but why in tunket did you burn—"

"I had to get out." She paused, glancing at Scott, and then asked, "Will they fight, George? Anybody but you?"

Vance pulled at his mustache, sharp blue eyes swinging from Scott to Yates to Bemis and then coming back to Patsy. "I heard about Tally getting knocked on his hunkers and some stranger standing up to Jimmy Kane. You got that feller here?"

Patsy jabbed a thumb at Scott. "Him."

Vance's mouth curled in a grin under his mustache. "I'm right proud to meet you, mister. Yes, sir, I think we'll all fight with a leader and a plan that might work. You've got a leader. What about a plan?"

"We've got it," Patsy said.

"Then I'll go hitch up and start after them hens of your'n." He frowned. "But I dunno about Jay. He ain't gonna cotton to our coming in on—"

"We'll be riding," Patsy interrupted. "We'll see you tonight."

Patsy wheeled her horse and rode off, angling southwest. Scott touched his black up and came abreast of her. "Struck me that Vance was pretty sure Runyan wouldn't like your dropping the meeting into his lap."

"I'll handle Jay," she said curtly.

"I was wondering why Vance settled up here if this valley has got so much grass. Don't look smart."

"It isn't. George isn't smart." She glanced at him, smiling a little. "I mean, he isn't smart the way most folks judge smartness. He's not much on working, either. He'd rather hunt and fish. He never worries about anything."

"But if he's got a few cows—" Scott began.

"They get along. George figures they will, anyhow. I guess he picked this spot because there's a spring just above the cabin, and, being close to the timber, he figured he could get a deer when he wanted one." She glanced at him again. "But there's one thing about George. He's not afraid of anything. He's not even afraid to die. And, even with all their hard luck, I think he's the happiest man in the valley."

Scott let it drop then, but he could understand why Vance had been unable to get his neighbors to follow him into a fight with Bengogh. Patsy's father perhaps had been much the same kind of man. He understood, too, why Jay Runyan's support was so important.

It was not yet midmorning when they rode into the Triangle R yard. Runyan's spread had the appearance of a small but prosperous place, a man's ranch which had been planned for work rather than comfort. It was not new, and Scott remembered Patsy had said he had settled here several years before, thinking everyone else would settle down around the lake.

When they reined up in front of a log house a man was spreading gravel in one of the corrals. He waved, and Patsy called, "Morning, Jay." The man straightened and leaned on his shovel handle, eyeing them with tentative aloofness.

"Sally's here," Patsy said. "Leastwise that's her horse in the far corral."

"I'll go see," Scott said, stepping down. "Maybe she's baking bread again."

Patsy winked at Yates and Bemis. "You boys stay out from underfoot. I'll talk to Jay." And she rode on toward the corral.

Scott walked up the path, leaving Bemis and Yates in their saddles in front of the house. He knocked, and a moment later Sally opened the door. For a moment she stood there motionless, staring blankly at him as if he were the last man in the world she expected to see.

He took off his hat. "I keep wondering, ma'am, if that bread ever got baked."

She laughed. "I finally took it out of the oven.

Come in. My conscience has been hurting me, Mr.—"

"Travis. Scott Travis. You know, ma'am, an eager conscience is a burden to carry."

"I meant I should have given you something to eat." She motioned toward a chair. "But I'm not baking this morning. I came out yesterday, and I've been cleaning house for my brother ever since."

He sat down, holding his hat awkwardly in front of him. "I just wanted to tell you something." He cleared his throat, wishing he had taken time to shave. "Coming in across the desert like I done, it was mighty good just to look at you and see what a house was like again. I mean, a nice house like yours. I ain't much on words—"

His voice trailed off, and she said gently, "You're doing real well, Mr. Travis."

"Scott, ma'am. To my friends."

She had taken the chair across from him, and now she began to rock, her hands folded on her lap. She was ill at ease. It was evident that she had not expected company, for she wore a faded-gingham dress and there was a dirt smudge across one cheek. Her dark hair was loosely knotted on the back of her head, and now she raised a hand in a quick, embarrassed motion to brush a stubborn lock away from her forehead.

In the moment of awkward silence panic crowded Scott. This was no way to start off with a woman, particularly a special woman whose respect he wanted. He thought of a number of things he could say—that he would like to settle here; that he was going to do something about this business of the folks who were trying to get ahead and Marvin Bengogh who was beating them down.

He might tell her his heart and soul went with his gun, but it would be on the right side, hers and Patsy's and George Vance's. Instead he reached for the makings. Somehow he couldn't put into words what he wanted her to know about him.

Suddenly she smiled, and the tension was gone. "You seem to have a way of catching me unprepared, Mr. Travis. First you ride up when I'm digging in the dirt. Now you find me in the middle of housecleaning." She motioned around the barren room with its meager furniture. "Jay just eats and sleeps here. If I didn't come out and clean up once in a while—"

"I'm sorry, ma'am." He rose. "Patsy said you'd be here, and I just wanted—"

"Sit down, Mr. Travis. It doesn't make a bit of difference."

"Scott, ma'am. To my friends." He reached into his pocket for a match, dropping again into the chair. "Patsy had some business with your brother."

Her smile deepened, small dimples appearing in her cheeks. "That business is of long standing. He wants to marry her, but she's awfully harum-scarum and can't make up her mind. She will, though, if she can get over hating Marvin Bengogh so she has some space in her heart for loving Jay."

"I didn't know about her and your brother."

"No, she wouldn't say anything about that." She stopped rocking and leaned forward. "I owe you an apology, Mr. Travis."

"Scott, ma'am, to—"

"I know, to your friends." She laughed softly. "All right, Scott. You see, I thought you were another tough coming to work for Bengogh."

"Like Tally and Jimmy Kane."

She flushed. "It doesn't sound very pretty, putting it that way, but I couldn't tell, seeing you just once. Then Frank Hibbard told me what happened, and I realized how terribly wrong I had been."

"No, you couldn't tell," he said gravely, and

wondered what she'd say if she knew why he had come to Easter Valley.

"I want to thank you for stopping Patsy," she said. "It would have been a terrible thing if she had killed him. Not that he doesn't deserve killing, but Jay—well, he wouldn't have understood."

"I'm glad I was handy." He fired his cigarette, looking at her, and he thought of Frank Hibbard, who was the wrong man for her. "We've got something cooked up for Bengogh. A couple of my friends are outside. We'd like to stay in the valley."

She hesitated, then she asked, "What have you cooked up?"

"Sort of includes you and your brother." He told her about the meeting. "I dunno about going ahead without talking to you and your brother, but Patsy allowed there wasn't time. She's already started the Vance kids out."

Sally began to rock furiously, her fingers tapping on the arms of her chair. "I never know how Jay will take things like that. He says a person should look before they leap, and Patsy's long on leaping and short on looking."

"If you look too long you never get around to leaping," Scott said.

"That's true." She rose. "Let's go out and talk to Jay."

She walked across the room in quick, graceful strides, very feminine and desirable even in the shapeless and faded dress. He caught up with her on the porch, saying, "Patsy told me you were the teacher. Or maybe it was you."

"I think I did." She gave him a quick glance. "I don't want you to think I'm unhappy about my job. It's—it's just the unfairness of it. I have only a few children, but a lot of families could live here and make a good living if it wasn't for Bengogh."

Bemis and Yates had dismounted and were hunkered in front of the house, smoking. They rose as Scott and Sally came up. Scott introduced them, Sally shaking hands in her straightforward way. Then she called, "Jay, you and Patsy come here."

Patsy was inside the corral with Runyan, pounding a fist into a palm, and even at this distance Scott could see that she was violently angry. Runyan hesitated when he heard Sally, then wheeled and walked out of the corral and came toward the house.

Patsy threw up her hands, shouting, "Jay Runyan, if you had four legs and longer ears you'd be a mule. You're that stubborn."

Runyan didn't look back. He came up, Patsy following hesitantly as if afraid to face the others. Scott, seeing the bitterness that shadowed her face, knew she had failed.

Runyan was a medium-tall man, stocky, with big hands and a wide pair of shoulders. About thirty, Scott judged, with a square head and jutting chin. He moved deliberately, and his first quick look of appraisal indicated to Scott that he would be a hard man to convince against his will.

"I reckon you're Travis." He held out his hand. "Glad to meet the gent that cooled off Wick Tally."

Scott shook hands, liking the man's firm grip and the way the brown eyes met his own. No fighter, perhaps, but a solid, careful man who would hold the respect of his neighbors.

"Glad to know you, Runyan. Heard a lot about you since I hit this country. Meet Shorty Yates and Ed Bemis. We're from Nebraska looking for a place to settle down."

"Reckon this ain't much like your buffalo-grass country." Runyan shook hands and turned back to Scott. "Now just what have you heard about me, Travis?"

"That you settled here in the north half of the

valley, that you're the only one living here who wasn't evicted from the wagon-road grant, and that you've got the biggest spread in the valley outside of the company's."

"That's all true," Runyan said with biting sharpness. "Likewise you've heard I could be a leader."

Scott glanced at Patsy, who had put her hands on her hips and was scowling at Runyan. "Yeah, I heard something like that."

"I've heard it a few times myself," Runyan said. "Now let's get some things straight. I don't want to be a leader. I'm not a gun fighter. I came here to raise cows. I am not in trouble with Bengogh, and, damn it, I don't aim to be."

"Patsy tell you what Delazon said about the company surrounding you?"

"That cattle buyer?" Runyan's mouth curled in contempt. "Don't mean a thing."

"It will," Scott said evenly. "You'll have a war on your hands whether you ask for it or not, and you'll be outnumbered so you'll have to move on or get killed trying to hold what's yours."

"I've told you the same thing," Sally said.

"Me, too," Patsy cried. "Jay, if you had the sense of a lame-brained, chowder-headed—"

"Shut up." Runyan drove his hands into his pants pockets and teetered back and forth on his toes, his face stormy. "I won't be pushed. When fighting time comes, by hell, I'll fight. But Patsy here goes ahead with her crazy scheme of getting our neighbors together. I can't stop 'em, so they'll be here tonight. But, damn it, don't look to me to back up your proposition."

"How long can you make out without driving a herd to the railroad?" Scott asked softly.

Some of the defiance went out of Runyan then. He lowered his gaze. "When I have to drive, I'll go through Bengogh's range. I ain't figuring on trying this fall."

Scott walked to his horse. "Might as well be riding, I guess. Got some business in town."

"Wait," Sally said. "Jay, there's one way to do this without having a lot of men killed. I've already started."

"So you're into this, too," Runyan said darkly. "I've got so I expect anything from Patsy, but I thought you had some common sense."

"I have," she flung at him. "I can see a little farther than the end of my nose, too. This is our fight, and it has been right along. If it doesn't come today, it will tomorrow; and the only thing we can do is to use the law."

Runyan laughed scornfully as if he considered this the most ridiculous thing he had ever heard. "Coming from anybody who knows Frank Hibbard as well as you do—"

"Don't say it, Jay." She gave him a frosty stare. "I've given up on Frank, so I wrote to the governor. We'll have an investigator here from Salem by the end of the month. Maybe sooner."

Runyan scratched his jaw, considering this. He said, "Well, now, maybe I'm wrong. I should have thought of that myself." He nodded at Scott. "Travis, I'll do some thinking on this afore evening. Meanwhile, I've got some notions of my own. We need to get a drive through to Winnemucca. No doubt about that."

"It'll take time to round your steers up," Scott said.

"Little early yet." Runyan turned to Sally. "These crazy galoots want to borrow money from Nolan to pay off some kind of a debt to Delazon."

Sally looked at Scott. "What kind of a debt?"

He hesitated, afraid that Patsy would tell the

story before she thought of the consequences. "He loaned us some money to get us out here," he said finally.

"What I want to know, Sally," Runyan said bluntly, "is whether you'll put your house up for security."

"We're not bringing her into this," Scott shouted. "Nobody thought of asking—"

"Of course I will," Sally broke in. "I'll ride to town with you."

Runyan swung to face Patsy. "Now I've got some orders to give you, Carrot Top. While Sally's in town you're staying here. You'll do the work of getting ready for your party and see how you like it."

She laughed. "Mister, I'll just take you up on that. You don't think I can clean house and bake pies, do you?"

"No, ma'am, I don't. All you're good for is to ride around and stir up trouble. Me, I don't think much of a woman who can't do something useful."

"You're in for a surprise." She thrust her chin at him defiantly. "I'll bake those pies, and if I can find the rat poison, I'll bake a special one for you. And don't call me Carrot Top."

"Oh, stop it, you two," Sally said. "Saddle my mare, Jay. I'll put on my riding-clothes."

"You're not going to slap a plaster on your house—" Scott began.

But she was already running to the house, and Runyan was walking to the corrals. Yates said, "Well, boy, I see what you were talking about. Wish I'd stopped at her house for a drink."

Bemis nodded. "That's quite a woman, Scott."

"And I wish I'd thought about writing to the governor," Patsy cried. "Maybe Jay's right about me. My head isn't good for anything but raising a crop of red hair." She bit her lip. "There goes my man, but he sure don't know it." She whirled and followed Sally into the house.

Yates snickered. "Say, this is gonna be some party. Rat poison in his pie. I'll bet she does it."

"Hope she don't cut my piece out of the wrong pie," Bemis said, grinning.

But there was no humor in this for Scott. He would not have come here in the first place if he had thought it would bring Sally into the trouble. He said somberly, "Wonder if she's gonna invite Hibbard out here tonight."

Chapter 10: Break-Up

THIS WAS THE MOST STARTLING THING THAT HAD EVER happened to Sally Runyan, so startling that she found herself unable to think of anything to say as they left the Triangle R. They angled southwest, Sally riding in front with Scott, Bemis and Yates behind, and presently they reached the road that led to Piute.

Occasionally she glanced at Scott, a strange tingle inside her that she had never experienced before. Then she felt a tightening in her chest. It was time she started thinking like an adult instead of a dreamy-eyed schoolgirl with her first case of puppy love. By this time Scott must have heard she was engaged to Frank, and he would have lost whatever interest he might otherwise have had in her.

No matter how she looked at her situation, it was a sorry affair. She didn't love Frank. She had thought so at first, but now she realized that it was pity she had felt, not love. He was a pathetic misfit who should never have come to a new, raw country like this. Now, staring ahead at the long sweep of the valley, she forced herself to admit something she had kept locked in the back of her mind. Frank would be a misfit wherever he was.

Again she asked herself the question that had been in her mind for months. Why had she said yes to Frank in the first place? She remembered the tired way he had proposed, the listless kisses which they had shared. She had always thought love did something for people—it should make life exciting and tantalizing but the two years she had been engaged to Frank had been neither exciting nor tantalizing. If a man was tired in his love-making, it seemed to her he'd be too tired to do anything well.

In time she had become accustomed to being engaged and had forgotten the first disappointment. She had patched and washed and ironed Frank's clothes; she had given him more meals than she could remember. Not once had she begrudged doing things for him but at the same time she had never adjusted herself to his lack of appreciation. She did what he expected of her but apparently it never occurred to him that there were a few things she expected of him.

She had fallen into a certain routine. Now she realized with a sudden and violent surge of rebellion that, if she kept on this way, she would eventually marry Frank and would end up supporting him. He could not possibly win another term as sheriff; it was not likely he would ever have a business of his own. He'd just go along, taking the easiest path he could find.

Then she thought of something else that seemed queer. She had never considered mortgaging her house to set Frank up in business. Last night she had asked Jay for a loan and he had flatly refused, saying she must take him for a fool—he wouldn't gamble five cents on anything Frank Hibbard wanted to do. But now Jay had suggested that she put her house up as security for the money Scott Travis and his friends wanted to borrow, and she had agreed to it without question.

She glanced at Scott again. There was a toughness about him that she liked. Perhaps it stemmed from the way he carried his gun and wore the old range clothes without apologizing to anyone, or possibly from his gray eyes and wide chin. Actually it was a combination of these things, she decided. Just as plainly as Frank Hibbard gave evidence of weakness, Scott Travis gave the impression of strength. Then she found herself wondering what his past life had been, and why he had come to Easter Valley.

They were within a mile of Piute before she made herself ask the question which had been in her mind from the time they had left the Triangle R. "Why did Delazon loan you money to come out here? I mean, did he want you to help him buy cattle or something?"

He gave her a straight look, hesitating as if he could not answer the question in the direct way she would want it answered. He said evasively, "No, he didn't need no help buying cattle. We knew him in Nebraska before he came out here."

Behind them Bemis said, "This business of owing Delazon anything is a lot of hogwash. Scott's just got too much conscience."

Scott did not answer. He was staring ahead at the town, his mouth a tight, down-curving line across his dark face. They rode in silence, the tension growing, and Sally regretted asking the question. She said lightly, "An eager conscience is a burden to carry, isn't it, Scott?"

He grinned at that. "Where did you hear such stuff?"

"From some old philosopher. Or have you ever

read the writings of any old philosophers?"

Shorty Yates snickered. "He can't read, ma'am. He got kicked out of school before he finished the first grade."

"Don't believe nothing he says," Scott said quickly. "Back in Nebraska, Shorty used to win the liars' contest every year, hands down. Why, even Ed didn't have a show, and Ed's considerable of a liar hisself."

"Well," Sally said thoughtfully, "it sounded like something Plato might have said."

"Plato?" Yates asked. "He live around here?"

She suppressed a smile. "No. He's been dead a long time."

"Who shot him?"

"I believe he died with his boots off."

"That's a fine way to die," Yates said. "Nice and easy, with a sawbones handy to give you pills so you can slip off unbeknownst to yourself."

"She's hoorawing you, Shorty," Scott said.

"I figured she was," Yates admitted, "but it's a pleasure to be hoorawed by a purty woman like her."

Scott glanced at Sally, his face grave again. "This business with Nolan was Patsy's idea. Chances are he'll throw us out of the bank. Anyhow, you ain't slapping no plaster on your house on account of us."

"We're all in this together," she said quietly.

"No such thing. It ain't your fight at all."

"It's Jay's fight even if he doesn't know it, and Jay's my brother."

She could not tell him it was Frank's fight, too, even though Frank would not accept it. Then she realized she had inadvertently stumbled on the reason she no longer loved him. She had lost her respect for him, and she could not love a man she did not respect. Only the binding power of habit had kept her from realizing that a long time ago. Or perhaps she had known it, really, but had been too stubborn to admit it.

If Frank had found enough courage to make a stand against Bengogh, if he had even made a reasonable effort to look into Pat Clark's death, she would have given him her love regardless of his other weaknesses.

Then Scott's words jarred her thoughts. "All right, it's your fight. But you ain't taking no chances on losing your home on our account."

They were in town then, and she said, "The least I can do is to go into the bank with you, but I want to go home first. I'll meet you in front of the bank in about fifteen minutes."

Scott nodded agreement, and she reined off Main Street and followed the alley to her house, thinking again as she had thought when she left town that her future relationship with Frank depended on what she found. She tied her mare in the barn and walked across the back yard to her garden.

The sickness of despair was in her then. The garden had not been watered, it had not been hoed, the carrots had not been weeded. She turned into the house and stopped just inside the kitchen door. Dirty dishes were still on the table. Frank had milked the cow, but he had left the morning milk in the bucket, the evening milk in the pan beside it. He had not even bothered to put it through the strainer.

For a moment Sally fought her tears. She had known she would find things this way; but still the hope had been in her that Frank loved her enough to do the few simple chores she had asked. If there had been any excuse it would have been different; but now she did not even try to think of one for him, as she had done so many times in the past.

She knew exactly what he would say. The dishes

wouldn't go anywhere. The weeds weren't very bad. Next week would be about the right time to hoe. And the watering? Why, old Gramp Banning who lived down the street was having his rheumatism again and that was a sure sign it was going to rain. No sense pumping all that water and toting it out to the garden when it was going to rain.

She couldn't argue with that kind of reasoning. No one could, and she wouldn't spend her lifetime trying to. If a man wouldn't work he just wouldn't work, and that was all there was to it. Without knowing it, Frank had driven the last shred of doubt from her mind. She would break off with him once for all.

She went into the bedroom and rummaged through a bureau drawer until she found the deed to her lot, knowing she should have broken with Frank a long time ago. There had been an accumulation of injuries like this through the years, but never anything that seemed to warrant a break. Now, as she left the house, a sudden fear was in her. When she faced him she would probably weaken as she had done in the past, weaken because these were still little things—too little, Frank would say, to make a fuss about.

Quickly she walked along the street to Frank's office, breathing hard, her blood pounding in her temples. He was at his desk playing solitaire just as she had found him so many times in the past.

"Howdy." Hibbard looked up. "What did Jay say about loaning you the money?"

That was like him. She faced him across the desk, staring at his gaunt face, the blue eyes that held no real hope. She should despise him, but she felt only pity, even though he had been the cause of so many fine dreams dying. She could not even put all the blame on him. The first mistake had been hers; she had been weak to keep on hoping when there was nothing upon which she could base her hopes.

"Frank, I think you should resign and leave the country," she said. "Today. Go back to the Willamette Valley where you belong."

He laid the cards down and leaned back, his battered old swivel chair creaking. "What's up?"

"Trouble. A lot of it. It won't wait until we hear from the governor. The little ranchers are meeting at the Triangle R tonight, and they're going to make plans."

"What kind of plans?"

"I'm not sure. Probably to drive a herd across Bengogh's range to the railroad."

He slammed a fist against his desk top, making the cards jump. "Why can't they let well enough alone? Bengogh ain't bothering 'em."

"He will. You know that." She put her hands behind her, fingers laced tightly together. "There's nothing holding you here, Frank. It's over between us."

She was surprised that his face showed no shock or disappointment. Perhaps it was her imagination, but it seemed to her he was relieved.

"I reckon I ain't the marrying kind," he said moodily. "You can go on teaching your kids. You'll be happier than you would be tied down to me."

"Will you leave the valley, Frank?"

He slumped forward in the tired way that was so familiar to her. "No," he said stubbornly. "Not right away I won't. If there is trouble I'll do the best I can."

She hesitated, wondering how many women had made the mistake of marrying men because they pitied them. Even fiery-tempered, Patsy might marry Jay because she knew he needed someone to prod him into action when his caution overpowered him but it would be wrong unless she loved him.

"I don't want you to get hurt, Frank," she said. "I'd feel better if you were—"

"I ain't leaving now." He bowed his head, absently nudging the cards with the tips of his fingers. "I'm sorry I didn't do them things you told me. I should have known how you'd feel, but a man's got to have some pride." His head jerked back, and he was suddenly defiant. "I ain't gonna leave the valley till I get a chance to show you. I know what you think, but you're wrong about me. I've had bad luck, that's all, just bad luck."

She whirled and walked out, and for some unexplainable reason there were tears in her eyes. She had never cried over Frank, and there was no reason for her doing it now. Suddenly she pictured him lying in the street, his gun in the dust beside slack fingers; she could hear the roar of a .45 crashing out into the silence, and she could hear someone say, "The fool! He shouldn't have tried it. He wasn't man enough to do the job."

The voice sounded familiar. Bengogh? That was it, Bengogh's voice; and over on the other side of the street she could see Jimmy Kane with a smoking gun in his hand, an inane grin on his lips.

She couldn't let it happen. Not to Frank who was so futile and so helpless. She found a handkerchief in her pocket and dried her eyes, and then she walked to the bank masking her face against the fear that pressed upon her heart. It was a strange feeling, for she had never really been afraid of anything in her life before; but she knew that Frank could not handle the trouble that was coming. Perhaps Scott Travis could. He was her one hope.

Chapter 11: The Challenge

SCOTT HAD NO INTENTION OF WAITING FIFTEEN MINUTES for Sally. He reined up in front of the bank and dismounted. As he tied, he said, "Let's get it over with."

Bemis and Yates stepped down, Bemis saying, "Gonna be a little different from the way we figured on meeting this Nolan *hombre*."

"A little," Scott said.

Yates flipped his cigarette stub into the dust and stepped around the hitchpole to the boardwalk. "Sally wanted you to wait—"

"Sally's staying out of this," Scott said sharply. "Craziest thing I ever heard, that fool brother wanting her to put her house up so we'd get a loan."

"You don't think Delazon will be here today, do you?" Bemis asked.

"I don't look for him," Scott answered. "After throwing lead at us last night he probably won't get within a mile of us; but I want the money in case he does. I'll feel better when he's paid off."

Bemis grinned. "You ain't doing this to impress the banker, are you?"

"He'll be a good man to have on our side," Scott said, and turned toward the front door of the bank.

"You can do the talking," Bemis said. "I just came along for the show."

Hank Nolan was sitting at his desk, clawlike hands clasped behind his head, eyes on the ceiling. He rose when he saw Scott, hesitated a moment as his eyes swung to Bemis and Yates, and then moved to the teller's window.

"Howdy, gents," he said in a cool, distant voice as if a little suspicious of their intent.

Scott offered his hand. "I'm Scott Travis."

Nolan gave Scott's hand a quick, firm grip, obviously puzzled. "I saw you whip Tally yesterday. I was one of them you said was wearing pants but wasn't a man."

Bemis laughed. "That was a mistake, Scott."

"No, he was right," Nolan said. "In five minutes he accomplished more than all of us have done in the two years Marvin Bengogh has been in the valley."

"Meet my partners, Mr. Nolan," Scott said. "Shorty Yates and Ed Bemis." After the banker had shaken hands, Scott added bluntly, "No sense beating around the bush. We're here to borrow fifteen hundred dollars."

Nolan stroked his goatlike beard, smiling gently. "That's quite a piece of money, Mr. Travis. What collateral do you have?"

Bemis laughed again. "Yeah, Scott. Tell him about our collateral."

"What we're wearing, our saddles, and our horses," Scott said, ignoring Bemis. "I know it's a lot of gall, coming in like this; but there's a little more to it. The people of this valley need help. We aim to give it, and we figure we'll help ourselves at the same time."

Nolan motioned toward the gate at the end of the counter. "A man with your gall always interests me, friend. Come on back. I'll listen to your proposition. When you're desperate enough, you'll listen to anything, and Patsy Clark has probably told you just how desperate we are."

Scott sat down across the desk from Nolan, his hat on his knee. Bemis and Yates stood behind him. Bemis said, "You ain't gonna hand out no fifteen hundred dollars to strangers like us. Just say so, and we'll be on our way."

"Your friend Travis made quite an impression handling Wick Tally the way he did," Nolan said. "I want to hear him speak his piece."

"We owe Delazon fifteen hundred dollars for getting us out here from Nebraska," Scott said. "He's supposed to be in town to collect. If he ain't here I figure we'll forget we owe it to him. As far as the bank's concerned you won't have nothing but our signature and our promise to stay in the valley till you're paid back."

"If we don't get plugged first," Bemis said darkly.

Yates kicked him on the shin. "Damn it, Ed, shut up, and let Scott talk."

"About this help you mentioned," Nolan prompted.

"Patsy told us how things stand," Scott said. "She got the notion of calling a meeting of the little fry at the Triangle R tonight. According to her, everybody's got beef to sell, but they can't drive across Bengogh's range to get their pool herd to Winnemucca."

Nolan nodded. "That's right. Bengogh has several armed riders patrolling the north boundary of the company ranch."

"But the law is on the side of the little fellows, isn't it?" Scott said.

Nolan laughed shortly. "In theory, yes."

"That's where we figured we could help. We'll take that herd and drive across Bengogh's range. Patsy says there's no money in the valley, so we allowed we'd take our pay in cattle and settle down here."

"You know what it will mean?" Nolan asked.

"Sure we know," Yates said; "but we figure we're about as tough as anybody Bengogh's got. It's a chance to make a stake, and right now we don't have much more'n the price of a drink between us."

Nolan leaned back in his swivel chair. "What does Runyan say? Or have you talked to him?"

"He ain't made up his mind," Scott said.

"If he makes it up the wrong way, gentlemen, you're licked." Nolan rose and walked to the window. "I don't savvy this Delazon *hombre*. I considered him a fake from the time he showed up here. He could go over on Crooked River and buy all the cattle he wants. Or the John Day."

"He is a fake," Scott said. "He's in cahoots with Bengogh. We didn't know that until after we got here."

Nolan took a pipe from his pocket and filled it, turning to face them. "Then why do you feel you owe him money?"

"A debt is a debt," Scott said. "You can't make nothing else out of it."

Nolan fished a match from his pocket, head tipped as he gravely considered Scott. "Perhaps Patsy didn't tell you that when Bengogh evicted the little ranchers, I loaned them almost all the money I had. I knew they were bad risks, but I couldn't let them leave the valley and have Bengogh win by default. I have some deposits from the townsmen and Runyan. If I loaned you fifteen hundred dollars, and there was a run on my bank, I'd have to close my doors."

Scott rose. "We might as well drift. Thanks for—"

"Wait." Nolan lighted his pipe, his eyes still on Scott's lean, wind-burned face. "You might make this drive without trouble. Bengogh knows that closing the road is illegal, so it may be a bluff. So far nobody has challenged him."

"If he ain't bluffing, he'll stop some lead," Yates said.

"The lead will be stopped by men like Tally and Jimmy Kane," Nolan said, "but not Bengogh. I'll tell you what I'll do. I'll be at that meeting tonight. If the boys, and that includes Jay Runyan, will play along, I'll let you have the money."

"Fair enough," Scott said.

"Don't make a mistake on one thing. If Bengogh isn't bluffing you'll have a hell of a fight on your hands. Bengogh's shrewd enough. I'll say that for him. He was in here yesterday trying to buy the notes the bank holds."

"You'd have enough cash to handle a run if you sold," Bemis said.

"I've thought of that," Nolan said, "and it is a temptation. I'm an old man with the good fortune to have a wife and three young children. I can't start again if I go under, and I probably would not be able to find a job at my age. Bengogh said it in just about those words."

"Hell, I'd sell!" Bemis said.

Nolan shook his head. "I can't. I saw the faces of these people when they were evicted. I gave them hope, and I can't take it away from them now. So you see my future as well as theirs depends on driving that herd to the railroad. If you could bring thirty thousand dollars back to this valley it would save all of us."

Scott, staring at the old man's pale, worried face, felt humbler than he had ever felt in his life before. He said, "I'm taking back what I said about there not being any men in this town."

Nolan took his pipe from his mouth, smiling gently. "I don't know. Sometimes when I think of my family I wonder how crazy I really am." Then he shook his head. "But after I go through hell for a while, thinking about Bengogh and how he's put a squeeze on us, I realize I've got to do what I set out to do."

"We'll see you tonight—" Scott began.

He heard someone come in, and turned. Sally walked toward them, her heels clicking sharply on the floor, two bright spots of color in her cheeks. She said angrily, "I told you to wait for me, Scott."

"You're not in this," he said.

She pushed the gate open and came to Nolan's desk. "You're not big enough to keep me out." She laid the deed to her lot in front of Nolan. "I have a little money on deposit here, Hank. I'll put that up for security along with my house." She gave Nolan a small smile. "I want you to loan these men what they need."

"You don't have to do that, Sally." Nolan pushed the deed back across the desk. "You could use that to help Frank start his feed store."

"There will be no feed store. Not if Frank needs my backing." She tapped the desk, defiant eyes on Nolan. "I'm going back to the Triangle R this afternoon, and I want someone to feed my chickens and milk my cow while I'm gone. Would you ask your oldest boy to do my chores?"

"Can't Frank—"

"No."

Nolan nodded as if he understood. "My boy will take care of things for you." He picked up the deed. "I'll put this in the safe, but I won't use it. The loan these men asked for will depend on what Jay and the others do."

Sally's gaze touched Scott's face. "They'll back them," she told Nolan. "They've got to."

"I'm not sure of that," Nolan said somberly. "Jay is a very cautious man. He may say that Travis and his friends will take the herd and not come back with the money. It may not be a pleasant meeting, Travis."

"Let's make it plain," Scott said. "Jay and all of them but George Vance are afraid of Bengogh. If they weren't they'd go along and see we didn't steal the money. Isn't that what you really meant, Nolan?"

"Yes," the banker murmured. "That's what I really meant. You can't give a coward courage."

"Jay isn't a coward," Sally cried.

"He'll have to prove it," Nolan said bitterly. "I've talked to him about this drive before."

None of them heard Wick Tally come in until he called, "Travis," in a loud, bullying tone.

Scott wheeled to face him. "Did you come for Delazon's money?"

"Delazon?" Tally gave him a mocking grin. "Hell, no! I don't run that gent's errands. I brung a message. Jimmy Kane wants you in the street. I came over to find out if you're as tough as you let on yesterday."

Tally swung around and stalked out. There was absolute silence for a moment, stunned silence while all of them thought about what this meant; then Scott drew his gun and checked it. Satisfied, he eased it back into leather, feeling sweat break through the skin of his face. He had brought this upon himself. Now there was no escape. He looked up, saw the worry and concern in Sally's eyes, and he thought, *She's afraid Frank Hibbard will get hurt.*

Nolan said in a low, fretful voice, "This is crazy, Travis. Can't you see what Bengogh's up to?"

Sally came to Scott and put her hands on his arms. "Hank's right, Scott. Getting yourself killed will ruin any chance we have to win."

"Shorty and Ed will be around," Scott said. "If they get any help they can take that herd through. If they don't get help I wouldn't make any difference one way or the other."

"But if you're dead they won't get any help," she cried. "Bengogh knows that. Jay and the rest will say look at what happened to you."

"This Kane?" Bemis asked. "How fast is he?"

"Plenty fast," Nolan answered. "Bengogh wouldn't have him on his payroll if he wasn't."

The cool indifference which had been in Bemis was gone now. He said, "If you don't get him, Scott, I will. That's a promise."

"Thanks, Ed. Sounds like you're changing your mind about things."

"Hell! If I'm in," Bemis said, "I'm in all the way."

"This is the damnedest thing I ever heard," Yates burst out. "Who do you two roosters think you are? You're cowhands, that's all, just cowhands. What gave you the idea you're gun slingers?"

"I never had the idea I was," Scott said. "What would you do, Shorty?"

"Nothing," Yates mumbled. "I'd go out the back door and keep on going."

"I don't reckon you would."

"But he's right," Sally urged. "It's just plain stupid to go out there and let Kane murder you. Stay here. I'll go talk to him."

Scott caught her by the arm and turned her around to look at him. He knew, then, that it was not Hibbard she was worried about, and the knowledge warmed him. *Funny*, he thought, *the way things go. You ride into town, and you see a woman. You stop and talk to her and a miracle happens, a miracle that changes life so that nothing is ever quite the same again.*

"If I live I want you to respect me," he said. "If I went out through that back door you'd never respect me. I might just as well let Kane shoot me."

"But just to let yourself be killed," she whispered. "It's so foolish. It's what Bengogh wants. Can't you see? He's counting on your crazy pride making you do just what you're doing."

"I think it's going to be all right," Scott said, and walked through the gate at the end of the counter and went on out into the sun-drenched street.

Chapter 12: Duel In Piute

SCOTT HAD NEVER EXPERIENCED ANYTHING LIKE THIS before. His mind was playing tricks on him, telescoping time so that many thoughts crowded through his head in an interval that ordinarily would have had room for only one.

He paused in front of the bank, noting that the street was deserted except for Jimmy Kane, who stood in the saloon doorway; yet only part of his mind was cognizant of this fact. The racing thoughts occupied the active portion of his mind.

The wasted, foolish years in Nebraska when he had been a cowhand little different from Yates or Bemis or any of the others—neither good nor bad, just indifferent; eating, sleeping, riding, getting drunk; bedding down with some floozy in Ogallala; not giving a Billy-be-damned thought about anybody or anything but himself.

The weeks in jail when nothing happened and the chance of dying at the end of a rope grew with each passing day. The terrible fact which he finally had to recognize that no one in his outfit cared about him one way or the other. He had given his loyalty; nothing had been given in return.

The long ride out here to Easter Valley. Seeing Sally Runyan, a pleasant island of time in an ocean of bitter indifference. Buying into Patsy Clark's troubles. Finding out what Delazon had been trying to do. And then the dream that had lain dormant for so long coming to life. He and Bemis and Yates could trade their guns and courage and trail savvy for a herd, a fair dream bright with promise. Now this ugly prospect of violent death.

The sun was bright and hot, glaring on the white dust of the street. Jimmy Kane had not moved. His probing eyes were on Scott, cool and confident while he waited for the tension to tangle the nerves of the man he planned to kill.

Scott felt the prickle of drying sweat on his face as other thoughts came to him—of Sally Runyan, who was worried about him and not about the possibility of Frank Hibbard being pulled into the trouble; of Hank Nolan, who possessed enough courage to gamble on three strangers who had come to Easter Valley to do a job that was the exact opposite to what they were doing now; of Patsy Clark and George Vance, who were not afraid of Marvin Bengogh.

People, ordinary, honest people whose lives had suddenly become tangled up with his. His victory or defeat meant happiness or misery for them. It was success or failure, it was life or death for at least some of them, all riding on the speed and accuracy of his right hand.

And why? Because a long-haired kid who had hired out to Bengogh was bound to take Scott Travis's life. Jimmy Kane was not important as a person; he was important only because he was a shield for Bengogh. If Kane died today, then Bengogh must die tomorrow or the next day, or the day after.

Scott walked around the hitchpole and stepped off the boardwalk into the deep dust of the street, moving slowly and deliberately, his mind focused on the job that lay before him. He was vaguely aware that men watched from windows and doorways along the street; then tension began to creep into him as Jimmy Kane had known it would; he felt a chill ravel down his spine, and he wondered if the watchers could hear the sound of his breathing.

He knew now he could not wait Kane out. As young as the gunman was, this was an old game to him. Scott called, "I hear you wanted to see me," his voice clear and challenging and without the slightest hint of the feeling that was in him.

Kane laughed, a brittle, taunting sound. "You're damned right I did. I told you this country was too hot for you, but you wasn't smart enough to take my advice. Now you're getting burned, mister."

Kane strode along the boardwalk until he reached the end of the horse trough, moving swiftly in catlike strides as if suddenly impelled to finish the job he had been so slow starting. Scott, standing there in the dust, right hand an inch from gun butt, knew he could not match Kane's speed. A gun was no stranger to him; he was accurate but not particularly fast. Shorty Yates had been right. He was a cowhand, not a gun slinger.

He called, "Wait, Kane." He saw in Kane's sudden haste a weakness he had not sensed was there, and he changed his mind about playing it out. An idea had come to him—an idea and a memory—and he knew that time, if used properly, would favor him.

Jimmy Kane stood motionless, plainly puzzled. A queer feeling worked into Scott, the haunting, weird feeling that he had watched this same scene in Ogallala when the town had been crammed at shipping-time with cowhands, cattle buyers, and the riffraff that crowd a railroad town at such a time—the same scene except that it had been two other men, one a cowboy, the other a professional gunman, and the gunman had died. And Scott remembered how it had been.

"Wait, hell!" Kane called. "Too late for waiting unless you tuck your tail and run."

"I ain't tucking my tail," Scott said. "I was just wondering if you were ready to meet your Maker."

The brittle laugh broke out of Kane again. "I've got lots of time. You're the one who had better be ready, friend."

"You're wrong, Kane. You're committing suicide." Then, fully aware of the gamble he was taking, Scott took his eyes off Kane and turned his head a trifle toward the sheriff's office. He called, "All right, Vance. Let him have it."

Kane's hand had already started downward as Scott's words hit his ears; he gripped the handle of his gun and drew, a motion that had been started and could not be stopped. He was by nature suspicious, and instinctively he turned his head to see if George Vance was really there. His gun swung clear of leather; he threw a shot at Scott, but the backward motion of his head had spoiled his aim and the bullet was wild.

Scott was pulling his walnut-handled .44 as the report of Kane's gun beat into the silence and was thrown back from the false fronts that lined the street; then two more shots rolled out close together, and Scott felt the white-hot burn of Kane's second bullet as it dug a furrow along his side under his left arm.

Kane stood there a moment, his legs spread, gun barrel slanted downward, mouth sprung open. Somehow he found the strength to bring his gun level again; but he did not pull the trigger. Scott fired, and this time he knocked Kane off his feet. He went down into the dust, his hat coming off and his long hair falling around his face; he brought himself up to his hands and knees, and reached a trembling hand for the gun he had dropped.

"Hold it, Kane." Scott ran toward him. "Hold it, or I'll give it to you again."

Blood was a wet, dark spot on Kane's shirt, and scarlet froth was on his lips; his face had the look of death. He held himself that way for a moment, the tip of his tongue touching his lips; he tried to say something, but time had run out for him. He fell back into the dust; his body twitched, and then he lay still, a twisted grotesque shape.

They burst out of the buildings along the street, Wick Tally and the barkeep out of the saloon, Hibbard from the sheriff's office, Bemis, Yates, Nolan, and Sally from the bank, and others Scott did not know. One was a doctor, black bag in hand, and he shouted in an important voice, "Get back, boys. Get back, and let me have a look at him."

Bemis slapped Scott on the back, crowing, "Just a cowhand, is he, Shorty? He ain't no gun slinger, you say."

"Hell, we saw that trick pulled in Ogallala." Yates gave Scott a crooked grin. "But it took guts to try it."

The doctor was on his feet. "Dead as he'll ever be. Lug him over to my office. Tally, tell Bengogh to come and get the carcass if he wants to bury Kane out there."

Scott felt Sally tug at his arm, and suddenly he was aware that he still held his gun. He put it into leather, and she was in his arms, crying. He held her close, whispering, "It's all right, Sally. It's all right just like I said it would be."

She clutched him frantically as if she could not believe it was true. "They'll help you now, Scott. Jay will. I know he will. You'll have all the men you need to take a pool herd across Bengogh's range."

Hank Nolan, watching them carry Kane's body

toward the doctor's office, heard what she said and nodded. "I think they will, Travis."

Frank Hibbard came then, walking slowly in his tired way. Scott looked at him over Sally's head, asking, "What do you call it, sheriff?"

Sally jumped back and turned. Hibbard took a long breath, staring at her as if Scott did not exist, and for a moment he was unable to say anything.

"You saw it, Frank," Sally cried. "You saw all of it. There's only one thing you can call it."

Hibbard brought his gaze to Scott and gave him a short nod. "I reckon it was justifiable homicide." He blinked and shook his head as if still unable to comprehend fully what had happened. "I knew you were bad medicine the first time I laid eyes on you. I wish to hell you'd kept on riding." Turning, he plodded back to his office.

The drum of hoofs came to Scott, and he looked up the street. Delazon was leaving town in a wild, headlong run, quirting his horse at every jump. Scott glanced at Bemis. He said dryly, "Didn't know he was in town."

"He ain't hanging around for his dinero," Bemis said.

The crowd had drifted away, all but Wick Tally, who stood motionless, defiant eyes on Scott as if he had half a mind to take up Kane's fight.

"How about it, mister?" Scott asked. "You want to play the hand out?"

Tally shook his head. "Not today. But I'll tell you one thing. Bengogh ain't one to let this go. This country's gonna be a damned-sight hotter now than it was before you drilled Jimmy."

"And it'll be hotter for Bengogh." Sally's lips were tight, pale, and her chin was thrust at him belligerently. "You tell Bengogh something for me. I've written to the governor, and I've told him what's going on here. Bengogh can guess what will happen if he keeps on holding land that doesn't belong to the company."

"I'll tell him," Tally said, and wheeled away.

Yates saw the blood on Scott's shirt. He shouted, "You're hit. Where the hell is that medico?"

"In his office," Sally cried. "Scott, why didn't you tell us?"

"Ain't much," Scott said, "but maybe he'd better have a look at it."

Sally gripped his arm. "I'm going back to the house. There are a few things I have to do, but I'll be ready to ride in an hour or so."

"Might as well tag along with you." Scott grinned at her. "Just to see you get back to the Triangle R. Meanwhile we'll get a drink, and maybe I'll have time to buy a shave."

"All right, Scott," she said, and walked away.

The doctor took only a minute to clean and bandage Scott's wound. "Just lost a little hide," he said. When he was done, he pinned gray eyes on Scott. "I was in the crowd yesterday when you cooled Tally off. I heard what you said about there not being any men in this burg." He squared his shoulders, scowling. "There's different kinds of men, mister. You're one and I'm one. Hank Nolan's another. We each do what we can, using whatever talents we have. Savvy?"

"I savvy a lot of things I didn't then," Scott said. "How much do I owe you?"

"Not a cent. Any day in the year that you can smoke down one of Bengogh's men, I'll patch you up free and be glad to do it." He glared at Scott. "But you ain't out of the woods yet. I don't know where you came from and what fetched you here. I don't know what you're up to, and I don't know anything about these two strangers you've got with you; but I'll tell you one thing I do know. Bengogh will get you in some tricky way you're not looking for."

"Thanks, doc." Scott left the office with Bemis and Yates.

They had a drink, the bartender serving them silently in the aloof way of one who wanted it clearly understood he was not taking sides. Scott stood at the bar, feeling the sting from his wound. He was still sweating, and he was weak and a little sick. The whiskey seemed to have no effect on him.

Yates was silent, turning his glass absent-mindedly with his finger tips, but Bemis understood. He said softly, "I know how you feel, boy. There's only one way to look at it. Kane wasn't worth a damn. Everybody's better off with him dead."

Scott nodded and tossed a coin on the bar top. "Let's go see about that shave."

"And some grub," Bemis said. "I'm holler clean down to my boot heels."

But there was no shave for Scott that day. As they left the saloon, they saw George Vance careen into the street, his rig taking the corner on two wheels. In that first glance Scott caught the anger that was riding the man, and he saw that the team had been driven hard.

"Now what?" Bemis grunted. Stepping to the edge of the walk, he shouted, "Vance."

Vance saw them and yanked on the lines. He pulled over to the edge of the walk and stopped in front of them, dust rolling up in a white cloud. Then he saw Hibbard come out of his office and yelled, "Frank, what are you gonna do about some thieves?"

"What thieves?" Hibbard asked wearily.

"Chicken thieves," Vance bawled. "That's what."

Hibbard threw up his hands. "George, I've got trouble. I don't feel like joshing."

"I ain't joshing," Vance shouted, so angry he was trembling. "Damn you, Frank, you'd go after horse thieves, wouldn't you? Or cattle rustlers?"

"Sure. But chicken thieves!" Hibbard shrugged. "Purty small potatoes, ain't it?"

"Not to me it ain't. I've lost my home to Bengogh, and I had to start over. I need everything I can get to keep my family from starving, and I was counting on Patsy's hens. She told me to go get 'em, but when I got there they was gone."

"Coyotes," Hibbard said.

"Two-legged ones. I can read sign." Vance's mustache bristled more belligerently than ever. "Three of 'em. Yesterday, I'd say. Feathers all over the pen and not a single hen left. Patsy, she said I could have 'em and pay her when I got it. Now they're gone."

"Maybe you know who took 'em," Hibbard sneered.

"Sure I know. It was Bengogh. Or some of his riders."

Hibbard laughed. "You trying to tell me that a man like Bengogh would steal chickens? George, you're loco."

"No, I ain't. I don't know why he done it, but it had to be him. Couldn't be nobody else."

"You get some proof, George, and I'll go get Bengogh. Until you have some, shut up." Hibbard wheeled and stalked back into his office.

Vance stared after him helplessly. "That's like him," he breathed. "If he ain't a hell of a star toter! Well, I'll go see Bengogh myself."

"And get yourself plugged," Bemis said. "Them chickens ain't worth it, Vance."

"They are to me." Vance blew out a long breath, the tips of his mustache quivering. "But it ain't that. You pile enough on a man, and he's got to do something. Well, I've had enough."

Scott, studying the man, sensed that nothing could stop him, and he would accomplish nothing by it. They would need George Vance tonight. And this would give Scott a reason to see Bengogh. Now that Jimmy Kane was dead, Bengogh might not be quite so certain of himself. It was possible that some sort of deal might be made about driving a herd across his range—not probable, but possible.

"I'll go with you," Scott said. "Put your team in the livery stable and get a saddle horse. That is, if you really want them hens back."

"You're damned right I do," Vance said eagerly, and drove on down the street.

Bemis grabbed Scott's arm. "You've done a job today," he shouted. "Let your luck stand."

Scott shook his head. "If Vance goes alone, he'll be killed."

"If you go, you'll both get beefed," Bemis bellowed. "Use your brain if you've got one."

"Let's say I don't have one. Ed, you know a man can't stand on his luck. If you get a gent like Bengogh back on his heels, you'd best keep swinging. That's what I aim to do. See that Sally gets home."

Ignoring Bemis's and Yates's belittling remarks about his intelligence, he strode toward his horse.

Chapter 13: A Woman's Heart

SALLY SAT DOWN THE INSTANT SHE REACHED HER house. Her legs would not have carried her another step. She had never let her nerves rule her; she had been strong because a woman must be strong to live in a new, raw country, and she had always taken pride in her strength. Suddenly she began to cry.

She hated weakness. When she had thought she loved Frank Hibbard, she had despised his tendency to dodge an issue and take the easy way out. That was probably the reason she had been able to break with him at last. She considered crying a weakness, and now she hated herself for it; but she could not stop.

She had no knowledge of time. She sat hunched forward in her chair, her body shaking with her sobs; then it passed, and she realized it was not weakness that had brought this on. It was sheer relief. The fact that Scott Travis was alive was a miracle brought about by a display of courage that was greater than any she had ever seen before.

She rose and went into the kitchen and built a fire. She took water and grain to her chickens; she watered her cow and forked hay into the manger, doubting that Frank had done either while she had been away.

When she returned to the house the teakettle was singing, and she washed and dried the dishes. She strained the milk, poured it into pans and left them in the pantry. It would clabber before she could use it, and so she would have to make cottage cheese out of some of it and give the rest to her hens.

The work was mechanical, for her mind lingered on the thing Scott had done. It was exactly as Shorty Yates had said. Scott was a cowhand, no more expert with a gun than the average rider; but he had faced a professional, and he had won. Therein lay the miracle.

She wondered why he had attempted it, and she could not be sure. Pride, she knew, was an over-powering force in some men. Perhaps it had been with Scott. It was mysterious to her, this code by which men like Scott lived, and she was not sure why some men adhered to it as closely as they did.

Probably none of the settlers—not even her brother Jay—would have done what Scott had. Still, she was sure that the pride which had driven Scott into the street to face Jimmy Kane existed in Jay and the others, even if it was not so compelling a force.

Scott possessed something the others did not, something she could not fully analyze. She remembered the confident way he had said, "I think it will be all right." He must have been afraid. Any sane man would have been, but he had not shown it.

Thinking back over what had happened, she was convinced that Scott had a feeling of destiny. He had found something in the valley he wanted, wanted so much he had been willing to risk his life for it; and somehow he must have known he would win.

As long as she lived, she would never forget the brief moment she had been in his arms, strong arms that had held her close and had thrust all danger away from her. She had been unable to believe he was alive; yet he was, and she had promised him that Jay and the others would help. But would they, even now that Jimmy Kane was dead—particularly Jay, who was so cautious? Hank Nolan had not been sure. He had shown his doubt by saying, "I think they will."

Now, as she finished putting things away, she realized that her job was to force Jay and his neighbors into keeping the promise she had made. It would not be easy. George Vance was the only man she could count on.

Jay did not lack courage. He had demonstrated that many times. He was simply too cautious, never wanting to gamble if he could help it. She knew what he would say tonight when the time came—that he wasn't sure Bengogh's greedy ambition would bring danger to all of them; that they knew nothing about Scott and his friends, and they would be foolish to trust them with a herd.

Jay had a cold, logical mind that always considered his interests before anything else. Selfish. Well, Jay was that, all right. He was never inclined to risk his life unless he was convinced it was for his own good. She could threaten to walk out and never speak to him again, but that wouldn't do any good. Somehow she had to make him see that backing Scott was the only way he could survive. In the end it would depend on trusting Scott and his friends. She had faith in them, and that was another thing she had to get over to Jay—perhaps the hardest thing, for faith in other persons was not a matter of logic.

As she left the house and walked to the barn, she thought about what she could say, the arguments that would influence Jay. There was only one that might work. She would tell him his future was bound up with the others, that if Bengogh wasn't smashed now he would in time smash Jay.

She saddled her mare, a sense of impending failure settling upon her. Jay had always been stubborn, and the trait, like his caution, had grown with the years. Even his love for Patsy would not change him. If they ever married it would be on his terms.

She led the mare into the alley, shut the barn door, and mounted. She heard someone call, "Sally." Frank's voice! She did not want to see him; she had taken toc much time already. Scott and the others would be impatient; but a perverse sense of obligation to Hibbard made her answer, "Back here," and she waited until he came around the barn.

For some reason that she did not understand he seemed less tired than usual. He didn't even lean against the barn wall as he ordinarily would have done. He stood spread-legged, his gaunt face upturned, his eyes studying her.

"Quite a man, this Travis," he said tentatively.

She refused to be baited into an argument, so she nodded. "Quite a man," she agreed.

"You're in love with him, ain't you?"

She was angry then, perhaps because it was true; but she denied it, shouting at him, "You're crazy. How could I be in love with a man I've seen only a few times?"

"I was wondering that myself," he said, "but I saw what happened. You came out of the bank, and he put his arms around you. You liked it. I ain't blind."

She had her anger under control then. She said evenly, "I'm not so sure about whether you're blind or not, Frank. It was just that I thought Kane would kill him. I—I was glad he was alive."

"Yeah, I reckon you were. I suppose you figure he'll go after Bengogh now."

"He will when the time comes."

Hibbard took a long breath. "Sally, I ain't begging for your love or for you to take me back. Maybe we never was in love with each other. I don't know. We kind of drifted into it, and all the time I knew I couldn't measure up to what you thought your man oughtta be."

She had never heard him talk like that before. She asked, "What are you trying to say, Frank?"

"This country will never be the same again," he said somberly. "It's partly that Kane's dead, and Kane was Bengogh's top gun hand. But there's something else. You feel it all over town. We were getting along without no real trouble, but now we'll have it."

"It was bound to come, Frank."

He shook his head. "Not like this. Before, Bengogh was solid. He'd built himself up so nobody thought he could be licked. He's worked on it ever since he drove the company herd into the valley. A few like George Vance and Pat Clark talked against him, but they never got anywhere."

"You are blind, Frank. You would never admit that Bengogh was wrong."

"Right or wrong, he held the big cards. Now he don't hold all of 'em." Hibbard fingered his star absently. "Well, I aim to find out why Travis is here, and where he came from and what he means to do."

"Ask him."

"I thought maybe you knew."

"Not all of it."

He scratched his nose, hesitating. Then he said, "Sally, I ain't afraid to die. I think my trouble has been that I was always afraid to live. I reckon it's a good thing we've busted up, because I got to leaning on you. Now I've got just myself. No friends. Not a real friend in the valley."

She put a hand out and dropped it, feeling again the pity she had for him and then realizing he was working on that pity. She said, "This is no good, Frank."

"I just want to make one thing clear. I ain't leaving the country like you asked me. I aim to be sheriff, and I'm caught in the middle in a hell of a squeeze. The company's got some rights. I've got to think of that, too."

She gripped the saddle horn, staring at him; and, in spite of herself, she was touched by what she saw in his face. Regret, perhaps, for what was lost and could not be regained. He was right about leaning on her. Now he might find the courage and confidence which had been so lacking in him. She hoped he would.

"Do what you think is right, Frank," she said softly.

"I will," he said, "but I'm asking one thing. Don't let Travis start trouble. Just let it ravel out. Then we'll see." He gave her a small grin and could not keep from adding, "Providing he's still alive by night."

"What do you mean by that?" she asked, a new fear beginning to nag her.

"You'll see. Sally, I want you to be happy. Don't marry Travis until you're sure he's good enough for you."

"Frank, I don't know why—"

"All right, all right. I know how it is with you and him. I reckon you see something in him you never did in me. Maybe it's his toughness—and damned if he ain't got it!"

"I told you—"

"I heard what you told me." His lips tightened. "Hell of a note when you stop and think about it. A fellow like him rides in, and everything's different." He snapped his fingers. "Like that. Well, we've all got an ax to grind, and Travis is sure gonna put a sharp edge on his."

Exasperated, she cried, "From where you stand, you've got no room to talk about him."

"Maybe," he said grimly. "Maybe not, but there's one thing you'd better know. If I find out he's wanted, so help me, I'll throw him into the jug." He swallowed. "Maybe he'll kill me, but I'm sure gonna try."

Hibbard swung around and strode away, his shoulders straight. She stared at him until he disappeared, realizing now that there was more pride in him than she had ever dreamed. Perhaps it was the reason he had refused to wash the dishes and do the chores she had asked him to; perhaps it had been his way of asserting himself. Maybe he had hated himself all this time for leaning upon her, and still had not been able to keep from it.

She rode along the alley and turned into Main Street, still thinking of Hibbard. She saw Yates and Bemis lounging in front of the store, but Scott was not around. Reining up, she called, "Where's Scott?"

"Gone to get himself killed," Yates said sourly. "We're supposed to see you get back to the Triangle R."

"I can get back without any help. Why didn't you go with Scott?"

"Didn't need us," Yates said.

"Where did he go?"

Ignoring her question, they mounted; and the three rode out of town, Sally between Yates and Bemis. Now fear for Scott's safety took hold of her.

She looked at Yates and then at Bemis. She said sharply, "I have a right to know where he went."

"You tell her, Ed," Yates said.

Bemis scowled and rubbed his chin. "Hiked out for the company ranch with Vance."

"The company ranch!" She stared at Bemis, unable to comprehend this. "Why, in heaven's name, why?"

"To see about Patsy's chickens," Bemis said.

"Vance claims Bengogh stole her hens. I tell you, ma'am, there never was a bigger idiot born than Scott Travis. Couldn't let his luck stand. He's got to go kick it in the teeth."

The alarm in her died. Scott was no idiot. He had a good reason for going with Vance, or he wouldn't have gone; and she had a feeling that he could get out of anything after what had happened today. She asked, "Has he changed, or has he always been this way?"

"Changed," Yates snorted. "Ma'am, he ain't nothing like the cowboy we knew. He was always satisfied to draw his thirty a month and found like the rest of us. We used to have a lot of fun together." He shook his head. "Now look at him."

Bemis nodded agreement. "I've seen it happen to other men. Like something had turned 'em inside out. I dunno what it was with Scott. Maybe just sitting in jail and thinking. A man gets into trouble when he thinks too much. Or it might have been after he got to the valley. Says he wants to stay here." He glanced at Sally. "Well, one thing's sure. He'll make his mark if he don't get plugged too soon."

"You said he was in jail." She ran the tip of her tongue over dry lips, thinking of what Hibbard had said about him being wanted. "Does the law—"

"Just a frame, ma'am," Bemis said hastily. "Scott never done nothing wrong."

They were silent then. Sally wanted to believe what he said, but he was Scott's friend. He might be lying. No, it couldn't be that way. It just couldn't. Bemis was telling the truth. Still, the doubt that Frank Hibbard had planted lingered in her mind and slowly grew.

Long shadows were riding beside them when they reached the Triangle R. Sally dismounted, handing the reins to Yates, and went to the house.

She caught the pleasant fragrance of baking pies the instant she came through the door. In the kitchen, Patsy was working at the table, sleeves rolled up, flour on her face and arms.

"Get your duds off." Patsy flashed Sally a smile. "I'm in over my head. But don't tell Jay."

Sally didn't move. She asked, "Why did Scott come to the valley?"

Patsy glanced at her, then picked up the rolling-pin and attacked a dab of dough. "Ask him."

"Do you know?"

"It isn't my business to know. Ask him, I tell you." Patsy looked up, gripping the rolling-pin fiercely. "But he's all right. Now you get busy and help me. We're going to feed everybody so much pie it'll be running out of their ears. I aim to show that mule-headed brother of yours."

"Scott shot and killed Jimmy Kane today," Sally said in a low voice.

Patsy straightened. "Well, what do you know about that!"

"And he went to the company ranch with Vance. They think Bengogh stole your hens."

"Don't tell me anything else. That's all I can stand." Then Patsy laughed. "I'll make you a bet. Scott will be back here with Bengogh's scalp." Then she squared her shoulders and added defiantly, "And I've got some news for you. Jay and me are getting married."

Sally walked to the girl and put her arms around her. "You sure?"

"Sure I'm sure."

Sally gave her a squeeze. "I'm glad. You'll be good for Jay." She paused, and then added gravely, "Patsy, don't marry him out of pity. Be sure you love him."

"Why, I've always loved him. Ever since I had pigtails which I guess I've still got. But Jay's so dad-blamed stubborn. He won't give an inch, and neither will I. We'll have an awful time, but it'll be fun. I'm going to give him a houseful of kids, and they'll all be redheaded boys. That'll fix him." She stopped and bit her lower lip. "Sally, why did you say that, about pitying him? That's crazy."

"I just wanted to be sure. I almost married Frank out of pity."

"You mean to tell me you finally broke it off with him?"

Sally nodded. "Today."

"Well, it's about time." She looked directly at Sally, and asked, "It's Scott, isn't it?"

Sally had been angry at Hibbard for saying that, but there was no use to deny it now. "Yes, but that isn't the reason I broke up with Frank. I just couldn't keep on pretending." She turned, calling, "I'll change my clothes and help you."

As she walked to her bedroom, she told herself it was none of her business why Scott was here. He was honest. The law didn't want him. She had to believe that; she had to believe he would come back from the company ranch whether he had Bengogh's scalp or not. He had to. So much depended on him.

Now, slipping out of her riding-skirt, she admitted to herself that she loved Scott Travis in a way she had not thought possible, so much that without him there was nothing. It didn't make any difference what his past had been. The future was what counted.

Chapter 14: The Big Boss

AS SCOTT LEFT TOWN WITH GEORGE VANCE, ED BEMIS'S words kept hammering against his ears. "You've done a job today. Let your luck stand." He glanced at Vance, who was staring ahead at the trace of a road that ran southward across the grass, and he remembered what Mrs. Vance had said. "Born to die young, George was."

For a time Scott struggled with his doubts, and he wondered if a man ever knew for sure what was right. He thought again, as so many times in the last hours, that he had never been faced with decisions like this because his life had been simple. Now there was nothing simple about it. For the first time he had a purpose; but the difficulty came in deciding how to achieve that purpose. No matter what happened this afternoon at the company ranch, he needed George Vance tonight at the meeting.

"You go back home, Vance," he said. "I'll find out about them chickens."

"The hell I will!" Vance glared at him, as proddy as a whiskery tomcat. "This is my chore. Them chickens was gonna be mine."

"I don't want to kick things loose this afternoon," Scott said. "I figure we'd better play it easy till we know how we stand with your neighbors."

"Then what are we coming down here for?"

"I want to see what Bengogh will do. I didn't get much chance to size him up yesterday."

Vance chewed on his lower lip a moment. Then he said reluctantly, "All right, you size him up."

"I was thinking it might get rough, and you've got a family—"

"That I have," Vance cut in, "but that ain't keeping me from siding with you. I know what you're up to, but it ain't gonna work. If we git plugged we git plugged, and that's all there is to it."

Scott grinned and nodded. Patsy had been right —Vance wasn't afraid of anything, not even of death. "All right, George." A queer man, this Vance—according to Patsy, the happiest man in the valley. Jay Runyan with his overweening caution would never be as happy.

"You know, Travis," Vance said, "I learned a long time ago that every man has got to live his own life, in his own way. Now you take Patsy's dad. Tough as a piece of rawhide, Pat was. Had plenty of savvy, too. Well, he used to say that a coward died a thousand times, but if a man had any guts, he only died once. He was always quoting from the Bible or Shakespeare or something."

"I wonder how many times Jay Runyan has died," Scott said.

"Jay ain't a coward," Vance said quickly. He was silent for a time, staring again at the twin ruts of the road that ran together and disappeared in the distance, smothered by the vastness of the grass. "Jay's just too damned careful. I ain't built that way. I figure like Patsy does. Her dad was murdered, and I aim to square it. The only way to do that is to get Bengogh. You done part of the job by nailing Jimmy Kane, but the trail leads to Bengogh no matter who held the club that cracked Pat Clark's skull."

"A man can bull in too fast on a deal like this," Scott said.

"Yeah, I know." Vance took a long breath. "That's my trouble, just like Jay's is being too careful. But I knew Pat like a brother. If he could talk he'd say he didn't mind the dying so much, but he'd hate like hell for nothing to come of it."

Again he was silent, his forehead creased in thought, and Scott could not think of anything to say. If he had died before Jimmy Kane's gun, Ed Bemis would have felt exactly as George Vance felt about Pat Clark. Most men would have taken advantage of the fact that they had families and turned back; but that was one thing Vance could not do.

"Pat used to say that the Lord moves in mysterious ways," he went on. "Us fool mortals just ain't smart enough to figure it out, and we ain't supposed to; but I've been thinking that maybe the Lord sent you here to do this job." He motioned eastward. "I had a little place yonder. Hated like hell to move, but I done it. Now it's plain enough that Bengogh ain't satisfied. We lick him, or we run; and damned if I'll run again."

Scott rolled a smoke. He sealed it and reached for a match, asking, "Why were you driving hell for leather like you were? Nobody chasing you, was there?"

"The devil was on my tail, I reckon," Vance said. "I was so mad I didn't know what I was doing. I kind o' hoped Hibbard would do something; but if I'd been in my right mind I'd have knowed better."

They had reached the east edge of the tule marsh, and the damp wind, blowing off the lake, brought the smell of the marsh to Scott's nostrils. From somewhere out in the grass to his left a meadow lark gave out its sweet song, and to the right he could hear the croaking of a blue heron. A strange and fascinating place, this valley. Here were two distinct worlds, grass and the lake, meadow larks and herons.

"Maybe I'm loco, but I keep thinking I may get back where I was. Pull a mess of trout out of the creek any time I wanted to. Shoot a duck or a goose. Trap some muskrats and sell the furs. Go hunting for egrets. Them plumes fetched a good price, you know. Didn't need to worry 'bout my cows long as I kept 'em from getting into the bog." He glared at the marsh. "Sometimes I wonder about a government that favors a man like Bengogh."

The same thought had poisoned Scott's mind when he was in jail, but now it seemed wrong. He said mildly, "It's our government, George. We get what we deserve."

"The hell we do! Take this Alec Schmidt. Started out with just his hands and his brain, and now he's a millionaire. A young purty wife, they tell me, but no kids. But me, all I've got is a family. You call that fair?"

"Depends on how Schmidt made his million. I'd like to see him."

"Maybe you'll get a chance. The talk is he'll be along. Might be here now." Vance glanced sideways at Scott. "You think maybe he don't like what Bengogh's been doing?"

"Maybe. It's why I want to see him."

Vance snorted. "You're barking up the wrong tree. He knows what Bengogh's been up to, all right."

Scott, knowing it was natural for Vance to be bitter but he might be wrong, dropped the matter. He was still thinking about it when they rode into the company headquarters, a big outfit, as he had thought when he first rode into the valley and saw the buildings from a distance; an impressive-looking layout that represented a great deal of work and a big investment. That was to Alec Schmidt's credit, or possibly Bengogh's.

Scott's eyes swept the stockade corrals and barns and sheds. There was no hint of activity. The only man in sight was Wick Tally, who lounged in front of the bunkhouse, wary eyes on the two visitors. Scott stepped down, saying softly, "Tally's yonder, but I don't see nobody else. Where do you reckon the crew is?"

"Out on the range," Vance answered. "Bengogh's got a good bunch of hands outside of Tally, who never has worked from the time he signed on."

Scott tied at the hitchpole in front of the house. "Delazon might be around keeping under cover. Keep your eyes peeled, George. I'll see if Bengogh's in the house."

"Want me to stay here?"

"No, come along. Just keep Tally off my back. If Delazon is around they might start the ball; but if Tally's alone I don't look for trouble."

They crossed to the house and stepped up on the porch. Scott knocked. The front door was open, and he could look into the big living-room. It was too big, he thought, and too well furnished for a ranch that had no women. He wondered absently if it was Schmidt's idea to have a ranch house like this, or Bengogh's.

Probably Schmidt's, he decided. A man of his wealth would want his house to stand for something just as he wanted his name to mean something—and again Scott wished he could talk to Schmidt. It seemed unreasonable that a man of his caliber would stoop to the things Bengogh had.

Scott knocked a second time, louder, and this time a woman came out of the back of the house, a tall, blond woman who moved across the living-room with quick, supple grace. He heard Vance say something under his breath. The woman was at the door then, smiling as she asked, "What can I do for you?"

"We want to see Bengogh," Scott said, and watched the smile dissolve as she sensed the feeling that was in him.

"He's busy."

"Not too busy. Tell him Travis is here."

She hesitated, her eyes turning to Vance and coming back. "I never heard him speak of anyone named Travis."

"Just tell him," Scott said.

She whirled and walked away. Vance said, "Must be Mrs. Schmidt. Old Alec's here."

"A good-looking woman."

"Yeah, for an old man," Vance grunted.

A moment later Bengogh came out of the office, his swarthy face affable. "How are you, Travis? I suppose you're here to be paid for saving my life."

The bald effrontery of this stirred Scott's temper. "You're wrong, Bengogh. In my book your life ain't worth a nickel. I'm sorry I saved it if it wasn't for keeping Patsy Clark out of trouble."

His words did not mar the mask on Bengogh's face. He said, his voice still courteous, "Then why are you here?"

Vance breathed, "Tally's coming."

Scott stepped into the room and put his back to the wall. He said, "If you want a blowup, mister, you'll get it. If you don't, send your watchdog back to the bunkhouse."

Bengogh smiled tolerantly. "Still proddy, aren't you?" He stepped to the door and motioned Tally back, then swung to face Scott. "I'm busy. If you have any business with me, say what it is, and get out."

"We're looking for Patsy Clark's chickens that you stole," Scott said.

For the first time Bengogh's expression altered, but whether from surprise or fear was a question in Scott's mind. Then the mask was in place again.

"I didn't steal her chickens. If you have any evidence that I did, go see Hibbard."

An old man came out of the office and stood

motionless, watching them. He would be Alec Schmidt, Scott guessed, and he was surprised, for the mental picture he had formed of Schmidt was entirely wrong. This man did not look like either a stockman or a millionaire. His eyes were bright and shrewd, but his face held the gray pallor of a sick man. Scott wondered if the fact that Schmidt was sick had anything to do with the tactics Bengogh had been using.

"Are you Schmidt?" Scott asked.

The old man moved to a chair and sat down. "That's right. Who are you?"

"Scott Travis." He motioned to Vance. "This is George Vance, who had a place near the lake till he was evicted."

Schmidt gave Vance a half-inch nod and brought his bright, piercing eyes to Scott. "What's this about chickens?"

"I'll ask a question before I answer yours. Do you know what Bengogh has been doing?"

"He's running this ranch," Schmidt said as if he were bored. "Now about the chickens?"

"Are you backing Bengogh in everything he does?"

"Of course. Marvin knows my policies. Naturally I would not put a man in his position unless I trusted him. Now I won't ask you again about the chickens."

"Patsy Clark was ordered to leave her cabin. She had a garden and some hens. Her father and mother are buried on her place—"

"All right, we'll let them stay buried," Schmidt said testily. "In time grass will grow on graves, and grass is the one thing that interests me—grass and cows, of course."

"And you don't give a damn about who gets hurt?"

Schmidt shrugged. "Look, friend. I bought the

wagon-road grant. If someone settled on my land and got hurt, it's his fault and not mine. I don't see that chickens or a garden or graves enter into the situation."

"You're a cold-blooded bastard if I ever saw one," Scott said. "Bengogh breaks the law. He hires professional killers to scare the settlers off their places. He has one of them murdered and makes it look like an accident. Then he steals a handful of chickens that belong to a girl, and you side him."

"Get out," Schmidt said angrily. "You'll keep a civil tongue in your head or get out."

"Not yet. We came to get those chickens."

"Go see the sheriff if you have any evidence."

"We don't have any evidence," Scott said, "but we know what happened."

"If you don't have any evidence you don't know what happened. Let me make one thing clear. We do not break the law, and we do our best to get along with our neighbors."

Mrs. Schmidt had come into the room from the office. She was very pale, one hand clutching her throat. She whispered, "Send him away, Alec. He's just a trouble-maker."

"I reckon I am, ma'am," Scott said, "and I'll make some more. I've got two things to say to you, Schmidt. Maybe you don't know it, but Bengogh's blocking a county road to keep the small ranchers from driving to the railroad. I propose to open that road and take a pool herd through to Winnemucca."

"By all means," Schmidt said. "We are not blocking the road."

Scott glanced at Vance. "You hear, George? He ain't blocking the road." He brought his gaze back to Schmidt. "Now the other thing. The schoolteacher in Piute has written to the governor that you're controlling land you don't own, so you'll have an investigation on your hands in a few days."

Schmidt shrugged as if it meant nothing. "I'm too old a hand at this game to be bluffed, Travis. Your teacher's letter will not bring an investigator to Easter Valley. The reason is simple, although you and your kind never understand it. A new country like this is for big men, not small ones. I'm a big man. When I move into an area I develop it. I bring money in and pay good wages. I'm an asset to the state and the county because I pay taxes. The authorities realize that."

Schmidt rose and went back into the office. Vance burst out, "Damn you, Bengogh! I want them chickens."

Bengogh had not stirred; his expression had not altered. He drew a double eagle from his pocket and tossed it to Vance. "It's possible that some of my boys took them, but not by my orders. Give that to the Clark girl. We don't steal chickens or anything else. We don't have to."

"Just land," Scott murmured. "Well, we might as well ride, George. We've found out all we need to know."

Vance gripped the coin, his knuckles white. He said bitterly, "Pat Clark used to say that a man reaped what he sowed. Remember that, Bengogh."

Vance wheeled and walked across the yard to the horses. Scott would have followed if Bengogh had not said softly, "Travis, you've played hell coming here like this. Before you go I want to make one thing clear."

"You and your boss have made a lot of things clear," Scott said.

"Not this," Bengogh said in a low, flat voice. "A man fights for what is his. Or if he works for someone else he fights for his boss. You were lucky with Jimmy Kane today. You will not be lucky again. I know why you came to Easter Valley. Take my advice and leave the country, or I'll see that everyone in the valley knows you came here to rob the bank."

"One good thing about advice, Bengogh," Scott said. "You don't have to take it. Now I'll give you some. Don't let Tally start throwing lead. Too many people know where we came this afternoon."

He walked out of the house, mounted, and rode away with Vance. Tally was still lounging in front of the bunkhouse, but Delazon had remained under cover if he was here. He might be in one of the barns or possibly in the bunkhouse, drawing a bead on Scott's back. Scott was not sure Bengogh would play it safe and let them go, for in his mind that might not be the safe way.

A prickle of fear ran down Scott's back, but he refused to give either Bengogh or Tally the satisfaction of knowing that it was there by bringing his horse up to a run. He rode slowly, glancing back only once to see Bengogh cross the yard to the bunkhouse. Then they were out of rifle range, and the tension went out of him.

"That was close, George," he said. "I was just wondering how it felt to get a slung in my back."

"They're slicker'n that," Vance said moodily. "Damn that Bengogh! Them chickens was gonna be mine, and I needed 'em. I can't eat a gold piece. I've just got to give it to Patsy."

"You were right about Schmidt," Scott said, "and I was wrong. Not much to choose between them *hombres* except that Alec Schmidt is smart and I'm not sure about Bengogh. I've got a hunch he'll make a mistake, and we'll have him."

"What are you gonna do now?"

"You hike on home and do your chores. I'm gonna take a sashay around by Patsy's place."

"Why?"

"Just a hunch. Maybe I can figure out that mistake."

"I don't like it," Vance said, "leaving you alone."

"We're safe enough now. George, you know your neighbors. Will they let us make that drive?"

"Depends on Jay Runyan, and what he says kind o' depends on Patsy and Sally. That's the way I size it up. Well, stay out of trouble."

Scott laughed. "I aim to. My backbone still itches."

Vance nodded and rode away. Scott cut westward and swung around the lake to Patsy's place, and then he was aware that two riders were following him. They were too far away to be recognized, but he had no doubt they were Tally and Delazon.

He dismounted, wondering what Bengogh's men meant to do. If it was a fight it might as well be here as anywhere, for there was no cover for them, once they broke through the screen of willows that bordered the creek.

For a time Scott stared at the charred remains of what had been the cabin, then turned his eyes to the fenced-in graves. Some things were clear to him now. One was the unmistakable fact that Alec Schmidt was a cold-blooded, dollar-seeking man. Patsy Clark's heartaches meant nothing to him. Probably he preferred not to know anything about them.

What the old man had said about buying the grant, and how the authorities would look at what he was doing, was probably true. To many county and state officials the fact that he paid his taxes was enough to make him an asset; and therefore he was one to be treated with respect.

Leaving his gelding ground-hitched, Scott walked around the garden and glanced into the chicken house. The door was open, and there were feathers on the floor just as George Vance had said. Probably Bengogh had hinted at the truth when he'd said some of his boys might have taken the hens, but not by his orders. Chicken-stealing was too piddling for Bengogh to bother with.

Scott went on to the shed and stockade corral, glancing eastward. The two riders had disappeared. They had had time to reach the willows and, having failed to make an appearance on this side of the creek, they must have pulled up to watch him. It seemed to make no sense at all, but Bengogh certainly would not have sent them after him without good reason.

Scott did not find anything of interest in either the shed or the corral. He returned to his horse and smoked a cigarette, studying the thick wall of willows. Now it occurred to him that he had to cross the creek to get to the Triangle R. When he did he'd probably run into an ambush.

He mounted and rode north, keeping well to the west of the creek. He would cross somewhere in the upper end of the valley where the willows were too small and thin to form an effective screen. Now, with the possibility of a bushwhack trap cut down to where it was not something to worry about, his mind turned back to his talk with Alec Schmidt.

Something bothered Scott about that talk, an elusive something he could not put his finger on. He had sent Vance on ahead because he wanted time and opportunity to think about the situation in which he had become involved; and now he found himself struggling with a thought that was as hard to grasp as a handful of smoke.

He recalled everything Schmidt had said; he remembered how Bengogh had been shoved for a time entirely out of the conversation. It struck him that Schmidt had backed Bengogh as a matter of principle, that there might be no real loyalty or friendship between them.

Obviously Schmidt would not want a stranger to see that anything was wrong between him and his manager. He had made a point of saying they did their best to get along with their neighbors; but now he knew that Bengogh was not getting along, that real trouble was at hand.

Scott crossed the road running east and west that Patsy had said led to the Columbia. He continued north, still keeping away from the creek; he tried to put himself in Schmidt's place, tried to think what the man's reaction would be when he discovered that Bengogh had stirred up a hornets' nest. It didn't work—he simply did not think the way Schmidt did; but he was sure the old man would be angry. To him anything that worked would be all right; but Bengogh's tactics weren't working.

The sun was almost down, and Scott swung toward the creek, knowing that he had to cross now if he was going to reach the Triangle R by the time it was dark. He spurred his gelding into a run, pulling his Colt and holding it in front of him, eyes raking the line of willows. Then, reaching the stream, he pulled his black down to a walk. Bengogh's men had not followed him, for at this point the willows were too thin to hide a pair of riders.

He replaced his gun in holster and put his gelding across the creek and up the bank. A moment later he reached the road that he had followed with Patsy the day before; he crossed it and rode directly eastward, the sun dying behind him and twilight moving out across the valley.

Lamplight bloomed in the windows of the Triangle R ranch house, and suddenly, for no reason that he could identify, Scott caught the elusive something that had been nagging him. There had been a vague hostility between Schmidt and Bengogh. He could not think of anything definite, but the more he thought about it, the more he was convinced he was right. His belief stemmed from the way things had been said rather than the actual words used, from the way Schmidt had taken over the conversation and treated Bengogh as if he were nothing more than a chore boy.

By the time Scott reached the Triangle R he had arrived at a decision. If his hunch was right Schmidt would be hard on Bengogh as soon as they were alone. Bengogh, anxious to get back into Schmidt's good graces, would be goaded into doing something that would force the issue. The smart thing, then, was to delay the drive to Winnemucca. They could afford to wait for Bengogh to make a mistake.

Chapter 15: Pattern of Murder

MARVIN BENGOGH STOOD IN THE DOORWAY WATCHING Scott Travis and George Vance ride away from the ranch. This was the best chance he had had to get Travis out of the way, perhaps the best chance he would ever have. From where he stood he could signal Tally to cut Travis and Vance out of their saddles. Delazon was hiding in the bunkhouse, probably with his Winchester in his hands, and would like nothing better than to put a slug into Travis's back.

Schmidt's presence limited Bengogh's actions. He would not stand for overt murder. He had made it clear too many times that he considered the indirect approach the best way to handle a knotty situation, and he had a long history of success behind him. He had a great capacity for using success to make success, and for that reason failure was one thing he would not tolerate. If Bengogh failed everything would be changed between them.

For a moment Bengogh stood with his hands clenched at his sides, cursing Travis who had come to the valley out of nowhere and had so completely ruined his plans. Travis was a hard man to kill. He was both lucky and tough, and that made him dangerous. Luck, to Bengogh's way of thinking, contributed more to a man's success than toughness. At the moment his own luck was bad, and Travis's was good. In time luck would change as a run of luck always did; but with Schmidt here he couldn't wait. Then, quite suddenly, he saw how this could be handled. If done right, luck would not enter the picture.

He walked rapidly to the bunkhouse. Tally had gone inside and was talking to Delazon when Bengogh stepped through the door. He swung around, accusing eyes on Bengogh.

"What the hell's the matter with you, boss?" Tally demanded. "We had that *hombre* right here in our hands, and you let him go."

Delazon was holding his Winchester. He leaned it against the wall, nodding. "I was right here at the window. Had a bead on his back, just waiting for Wick's sign. Now they're gone."

"I couldn't do it," Bengogh said sharply, "not with Schmidt in the house."

"Why, hell, if that's all—" Tally began.

"I know," Bengogh cut in. "That's how we've got to work it. Now I want you boys to saddle up and take after Travis. I just want him nailed down so he's alone. Figure out some way to keep him from getting to town for two or three hours."

Tally nodded, understanding what Bengogh had

in mind, but Delazon was not so fast mentally. He burst out, "Why in hell shouldn't we kill him? He's too dangerous—"

"You bet he's dangerous," Bengogh broke in, "and I can thank you for bringing him here. So far you've done nothing right, Sam. This is your last chance. If you bungle this I'll kill you. Understand?"

Delazon lowered his gaze. "I savvy."

"If you do you'll let Wick do your thinking," Bengogh said, and, turning, walked back to the house.

Ellen was on the porch; and when she saw him she called frantically, "Marvin, Alec wants you."

From the strained look on her face, Bengogh knew that this was trouble. The fat was in the fire. He might as well face it; but, within the hour, everything would be changed.

"What's wrong?" Bengogh asked as he stepped up on the porch.

Ellen gripped his arm. "He's mad. I never saw him so mad. I've always been able to handle him, but now he's crazy. I don't know what got into him."

"Don't worry." Bengogh went past her into the house.

"That you, Marvin?" Schmidt bellowed.

Bengogh had never heard the old man raise his voice like that, and for an instant a sense of disaster washed through him. This had to be done fast, and it had to be done right; and if he lost his temper his plan would fail. But he'd control himself; he'd let Schmidt have his moment.

"It's me, Alec." Bengogh crossed the big living-room to the office.

Alec was sitting at the desk, his blue-veined hands knotted. In the first glance Bengogh saw that the old man's face was mottled, and he was breathing hard as if each breath was a struggle. For a moment Bengogh considered changing his plan and letting nature do the job for him. He decided against it at once. There wasn't time. You never knew about a man's heart. Schmidt might live for months, or even years.

Ellen walked past Bengogh and stood at the desk, looking down at her husband. Usually she could control her emotions; but now she was very pale, and her chin was quivering. Something passed between them, Bengogh thought, and the last doubt about the wisdom of his plan fled from him. He had no time at all.

"Alec, you can't judge—" Ellen began.

"I can and I will judge." Schmidt glared at Bengogh. "I made the company, and the company made this ranch. I have never failed at anything I started, and I will not fail now. Go upstairs, Ellen."

"But you're sick, Alec." She laid a hand on Schmidt's shoulder. "You shouldn't get worked up like this. The doctor said—"

"To hell with what the doctor said! Go upstairs."

Ellen's gaze touched Bengogh's face briefly; then she flounced out of the room. Bengogh sat down across the desk from Schmidt, hearing the sharp, angry click of her heels as she crossed the front room and went up the stairs. He reached into his coat pocket for a cigar, knowing what lay ahead and hating the part he must play. Humility did not come easily to Marvin Bengogh.

"Who is this Travis?" Schmidt demanded.

"Just a drifter." Bengogh put the cigar into his mouth and began to chew on it. "Rode into the valley a day or two ago and managed to make friends out of some of the little fry like George Vance and the Clark girl."

"I could use a man of his caliber. Stood up and talked to me like I was just another two-bit rancher." Schmidt filled his pipe, eyes lowered. "He's the kind I've used to build the company. How'd you happen to let him get on the other side?"

"Hell! I can't hire every drifter who hits the valley. He doesn't look as big to me as he does to you."

Schmidt had put his pipe into his mouth. Now he jerked it out, his face growing darker with the fury that gripped him. He said hoarsely, "For a long time I've known you were a son of a bitch, but I didn't think you were a fool. You never pulled the wool over my eyes like you thought you were doing, but I kept hoping you were as smart a man as Ellen thought." He fished a match from his pocket, lowering his gaze again. "Trouble is, a woman never sizes a man up right when she's in love with him."

A coldness settled in Bengogh's belly. He seldom kept an unlighted cigar in his mouth, but now he chewed on it until it was a tattered brown mass. Fear was in him again—not the kind of fear he had felt when Patsy Clark tried to kill him, but the terrible fear that Schmidt, knowing the truth, would somehow manage to defeat him.

"I don't understand you, Alec," he said in a low tone.

"You understand, all right." Schmidt lighted his pipe and leaned back in the chair, his hands gripping the arms. "I've had you traced from A to Z. I know how Ellen met you, and how much Ellen saw you on the sly in San Francisco. I've seen the look on her face when she bragged about you and begged me to kick you upstairs. She thought she was fooling me, too, but she's as easy to read as a first-grade primer."

Bengogh jerked the frayed cigar out of his mouth and threw it into the spittoon. He could only say, "You're wrong, Alec," and knew it would do no good. They were on thin ice now. If he had any talent for acting, this was the time to use it.

Schmidt laughed shortly, a sound that held more misery than humor. "Don't lie to me now, Marvin. I know. I've known for quite a while. I know she was with you last night. The Almighty doesn't need to send me to hell after I'm dead. I've been there."

For a moment he teetered back and forth in the swivel chair, the knuckles of his hands white. Then he said slowly, "I should have killed you. I guess a younger man would have. There was just one reason I didn't, but it's a reason you'll never understand. I love Ellen. I know I don't have long to live, and you were giving her something she wanted and I couldn't give her; so I let it go. All this time I've hated you as much as I've loved her."

Bengogh rose, thankful again for the years he had spent at a poker table. The ice was getting thinner. He said evenly, "This isn't good, Alec. I've done a good job for you here. It hasn't been all roses, you know."

"A good job, you say." Schmidt laughed again. "Well, maybe it was a good job except for one thing. That's your relations with the settlers. Half of my success has been due to the fact that I always managed to keep the little fellows friendly. Even when I drove them from their homes, I kept them on my side. I gave them work, or helped them get a start somewhere else. You've failed, Marvin, just plain failed, and that's the one sin I can't overlook."

Bengogh moved to the window and stared out across the grass, confidence working into him again. Schmidt had waited too long for this blowup. Bengogh said, "I haven't failed, Alec, not yet."

Schmidt snorted his derision. "You even steal chickens. That's the most piddling thing I can think of."

"I didn't steal those chickens. I sent three of the boys to see if the Clark girl had left her cabin. They found out she'd burned it, but the chickens were still there, so they brought them home, thinking she'd gone off and left them. It was a mistake, but I didn't make it."

"That proves you're a fool," Schmidt said hotly. "If you hire men who make mistakes, the mistakes are yours. You've got George Vance steamed up. You've pulled this grub-line rider into it, and he looks to me like a pretty tough boy. You even got the schoolteacher writing to the governor. I have some political strings, but I doubt that I can pull enough."

Bengogh drew another cigar from his pocket and lighted it, knowing that all he had to do now was to placate the old man for a few minutes. Humility—that was the answer. He could afford to crawl now. He said, "Give me another year, Alec, and I'll have this all straightened up. I'll get to work draining the marsh. I'll make this the best ranch you own, and you'll be proud of it."

"I don't have a year to live." Schmidt laid his pipe on the desk. "That's why I shut my eyes to you and Ellen. I was counting on you because I didn't want Ellen to lose everything I'm leaving her. I kept hoping you were big enough to run the company, but you've shown me you aren't. You're a small man with a small mind. If I don't stop you, Ellen will marry you, and she'll lose everything in five years."

Bengogh walked to the desk. "Alec, you're all in a lather over nothing. You'll probably live another five years. Come back next summer. You'll have the valley, and there won't be any trouble. That's a promise."

For a moment Schmidt said nothing. He bent forward, one hand over his chest, his face contorted with agony. Bengogh watched with cool detachment, thinking that it would be very simple if the old man's heart quit on him now. He wouldn't have to go on with his plan. Then he wondered if Ellen knew how completely Schmidt had guessed the truth.

Schmidt straightened up and sat back in his chair, the pain passing. "No. You're fired, Marvin. I'll have another man come north as soon as I get to Salem and can send a wire."

"You're not being fair, Alec, but I'll stay as long as you need me." Bengogh drew on his cigar, thinking he had said that in just the right tone. Then he added, "Alec, I'll hitch up your team, and we'll take a ride. It'll do you good to get outside and breathe a little fresh air. While you're here I want to show you what I had in mind about the marsh."

Bengogh had a bad moment while Schmidt hesitated. Everything depended on the old man going with him, and he could not afford to make him go at the point of a gun. Ellen might see what was happening.

"I guess it would be good for me to get out," Schmidt said. "I'll start for Salem in the morning. You'll have to send a man with us. It isn't safe for Ellen to be alone with me in the condition I'm in."

Another idea gripped Bengogh's mind. He could send Wick Tally to do the job along the lonely trail between Easter Valley and Salem. No, his other plan was better. It would get rid of Scott Travis, too. Anyhow, he had depended on too many other men—men like Jimmy Kane who had failed him.

"Better put on your heavy coat, Alec," Bengogh said. "Might be a little chilly before you get back."

He left the office and went upstairs. He habitually carried a small gun in a coat pocket, but this called for a .44. He stepped into his room and, opening a bureau drawer, took out a long-barreled

Colt and slid it under his waistband. When he stepped into the hall, Ellen was waiting for him.

She had been crying. It was the first time since he had known her that he was sure she had broken down, and irritation stirred in him. This was no time for tears.

She came into his arms, clutching him with frantic urgency as if she was afraid she had lost him. She whispered, "What did he say?"

"Not much. He's sore about Travis coming and the teacher writing to Salem, but it will be all right."

She kissed him, letting him feel the passionate hunger that she had for him. A great satisfaction warmed him. For all of his money and power, Alec had never received a kiss like that from her. She needed Marvin Bengogh, not Alec, and that was probably what really got under the old man's hide.

He pushed her lips away, saying, "I've got to go, Ellen. I'm showing him what I want to do with the marsh."

She stepped back, her eyes on his face. "I thought he was going to fire you. I'd go with you if he did. You knew that, didn't you?"

"I hoped you would," he said, "but we won't have to worry about living on peanuts. It's going to work out like we planned."

He left the house and harnessed Schmidt's team, thinking out exactly how this was to be done. He hooked the team to the buggy and wrapped the lines around the brake handle; he caught and saddled his horse. Whatever happened, he must not alarm Alec. He tied his horse behind the buggy and, stepping into the seat, drove to the front of the house.

Schmidt came out, wearing his heavy coat. He motioned to the saddle horse. "What are you taking him for?"

"I thought you could drive back, Alec. What I want to show you won't take long. Then I'll ride over to the other side of the lake. I want to look at the calves. The boys are out there today, and I'll come back with them."

Schmidt nodded and stepped into the seat. As they drove away, Bengogh felt the pressure of the gun under his waistband. Nothing could stop him. A fool, was he? Well, Alec wasn't as good in his judgment of men as he thought. Marvin Bengogh was not a fool, and Alec would know that before he died.

"This business of draining a tule marsh is new to me," Bengogh said as if nothing had gone between them. "I'll have to experiment with it. Maybe take a piece of ground that's a little higher than the rest and run some ditches toward the lake. Then I'll burn the tules when they dry out. Of course ground like that is always subirrigated, and even in dry summers it will raise good hay. It will be a good investment, Alec. Just the cost of the labor."

Schmidt glanced at him, his face grim. "You're done, Marvin. I thought we understood each other."

Bengogh shrugged. "I've spent two years here, Alec. I've worked like a dog because I wanted to satisfy you. When I left California I swore I'd make this the best damned ranch you owned, and I've done as much as any man could do in two years."

"I'll admit that, but—"

"All right. Let me finish. With me it wasn't just a matter of drawing my wages like it would have been with some men. I did a little dreaming about the future, the sort of dreaming a man does if the ranch he's running is his own. I suppose that proves me to be the fool you claim I am. I wouldn't have done that dreaming if I hadn't trusted you."

Schmidt glanced at Bengogh again. The mottled

color had left his face, and it was the pasty gray that it had been when he arrived the evening before. He shivered as if he were cold, his hands shoved down into the pockets of his coat.

"I am not a sentimental man, Marvin," Schmidt said, "except when it comes to Ellen. Now that I've found out you aren't big enough to run the company, you aren't big enough for Ellen so you might as well save your breath."

"All right," Bengogh said. "Maybe I'd better pull my freight in the morning. When you're done with a man, you're done right now, aren't you?"

"Yes," Schmidt said. "I am. I guess it would be better if you left tomorrow. I'll pick out one of the boys to run the outfit until I can send a man north."

Bengogh's hands tightened on the lines. He wanted to tell the old man that, no matter what he did now, he would lose Ellen. He wanted to hurt Schmidt, to describe the way she had kissed him, the passionate love that had been his and Schmidt had missed. He wanted to tell him that the harsh things he had said this afternoon had been wasted because there was nothing Alec could do that would separate his wife and Marvin Bengogh.

But he said none of those things because it would have been only a cheap and temporary triumph. They were still too close to the house to finish this. He had waited this long; he could wait a little longer.

They were silent until they reached the edge of the tule marsh. Bengogh handed the reins to Schmidt, saying, "I'll get my horse."

He got down and went around to the back. He untied his horse, looking at Schmidt's back, bent forward a little as if he were tired. He mounted and, riding around the buggy, reined up beside the team.

"You brought me out here to murder me," Schmidt said wearily. "Go ahead."

Bengogh stared at the old man, his heart hammering with sudden violence. Schmidt had known all the time; but he hadn't been afraid, and he wasn't afraid now.

"How did you know?" Bengogh breathed.

"Because you're easy to read," Schmidt said. "You're a coward, Marvin, a cheap, filthy little coward. I found that out this afternoon when this fellow Travis showed up. You took what I had to say without a word, but all the time I could see in your face what you meant to do."

"Then why did you come?"

"It doesn't matter. The doctor told me not to make this trip, but I was too bullheaded to listen. I found out the last few weeks just how bad my heart is; so I might as well die with your bullet in me as wait for my heart to quit."

Bengogh drew his gun, unable to understand how Schmidt could take it like this, and burst out, "So you think I'm a fool as well as a coward. Well, I think you're the fool. You've made a fortune for me. What do you think of that?"

"I don't think anything of it." A small smile touched Schmidt's lips. "You won't get it, Marvin. That's the real reason I came with you. If I ran you off the ranch you'd get in touch with Ellen, and she'd go to you because she'd be in love with you. Now you'll lose her."

"You're crazy," Bengogh shouted. "She'll never know I killed you."

"Think not?" Schmidt's smile deepened. "You're going to be surprised, Marvin. When I'm dead I'll come between you, and that is something I've never been able to do alive."

Bengogh thumbed back the hammer and began to curse, letting his rage take hold of him. He fired twice, driving both bullets into Schmidt's chest, and the team, boogered by the firing, began to run.

The lines fell from the old man's slack fingers, and he slid forward out of the seat.

Bengogh slipped the gun back under his waistband, suddenly remembering he had forgotten to look around to see if anyone was in sight. Then the quick panic died. There was no one, nothing moving anywhere on the grass except the team that was running north. Quickly Bengogh reined his horse around and rode south at a gallop.

He would meet the crew and ride home with them. If Tally and Delazon did the job they were supposed to do, no one could be sure that Scott Travis had not done the killing. Both Bengogh and Ellen could swear that hard words had passed between Schmidt and Travis that afternoon. Tally and Delazon would testify that they had seen Travis riding north. Or, better yet, they could say they had actually seen the shooting.

On the other hand, if Tally and Delazon had not kept Travis out of circulation, there was still nothing to connect Bengogh with the shooting. No one, certainly not Ellen, would ever think of him. No, he was in the clear. Then the fear that Bengogh had lived with for so long began working into him again. Schmidt had said he would come between Bengogh and Ellen when he was dead. That was crazy.

If a man could ever be sure of a woman, Bengogh could be sure of Ellen. But why had Schmidt said that? Why had he come out here, knowing what Bengogh aimed to do? He must have sensed something about Ellen that Bengogh had never felt. Then it came to him. A man was never sure of a woman. Schmidt must have been thinking of the day when he had been sure of Ellen.

Chapter 16: Conference

THE WESTERN SKY STILL HELD A LINGERING TOUCH OF color when Scott rode into the Triangle R yard. Bemis and Yates were hunkered beside the corral gate when he reined up and dismounted.

"The hero's back," Bemis said. "Got any holes in your hide?"

"How would he get any holes?" Yates asked. "Chances are, he's been out gabbing with one of them there old philosophers Sally was talking about. They don't put holes in your hide, Ed. They just wear you down with their tongues."

"All right," Scott said testily. "Where's Runyan?"

"In the house." Yates got up. "I'll take care of your horse. You get into that house and show Sally you're all in one piece, or I'll bend my gun barrel over your noggin."

"Runyan made up his mind yet?"

"Ain't heard him say. Will you get into that house?"

Scott swung around and strode across the dusty yard, a little uneasy about facing Sally. She'd probably whittle him down with her tongue for going to the company ranch with Vance. He went in through the front door, noticing that the walls of the living-room were lined with benches made by laying planks across upended nail kegs. They must, he thought, be expecting every rancher in the north half of the valley.

Sally appeared in the kitchen door. She said, "Scott," in a low voice, and leaned against the jamb, her body limp. "Where have you been? George Vance came by three hours ago."

"Just took the long way around," he said carelessly. "I didn't figure anybody would worry."

She straightened, angry now that the momentary weakness of relief had gone from her. "We didn't, Mr. Travis, we didn't worry for a minute."

"Scott, to my—"

"If you expect to have any friends," she said sharply, "you'll start looking out for yourself."

He crossed the room to her. "Look, Sally. Me and George got away from the company ranch slicker'n a whistle. I thought he'd tell you so nobody'd worry about me."

"I don't want to talk about it." She whirled so violently that her skirt flew out from her trim ankles in a wide sweep of red-and-white gingham. "Sit down. I've kept your supper warm."

"I'll wash up," he said, and went on through the kitchen to the back porch.

When he returned Runyan and Patsy had come into the kitchen. From the bright color in Patsy's cheeks, something had happened here today. Runyan grinned a little self-consciously as he said, "Glad you're back, Travis. We was all wondering if you'd got your feet caught in a bear trap."

Scott glanced at Patsy, who lowered her gaze. Bashfulness, he thought, did not set well upon her. "Looks to me," he said, "like something happened around here."

Sally looked up from the table where she was pouring his coffee. "Nothing important. They're just getting married, that's all."

"It is important," Patsy flared. "It's the most important thing that ever happened in Easter Valley."

"Why, now," Runyan said, winking at Scott, "I

wouldn't stop there. It's the most important thing that's happened in the United States since the Civil War."

"Sit down, Scott," Sally said. "You'd better eat before they get here; and if you don't quit encouraging Jay he'll brag the rest of the night."

Scott held out his hand to Runyan. "Congratulations, Jay. You've got your loop on quite a girl."

Runyan shook hands, grinning. "Thanks. Only thing is I ain't sure who got whose loop on who. She's been chasing me ever since she could walk."

"That's not so," Patsy said hotly. "He couldn't wait till I grew up. If he hadn't caught me in a weak moment—"

"Weak moment, is it?" Runyan shouted. "Of all the dad-gummed gall! She got me mellowed up with a couple of pies, and I couldn't turn her down."

"Scott, your supper's getting cold," Sally said, "and we've got a little talking to do before the men get here."

Scott sat down at the table and began to eat. Runyan glanced at Sally, chewing on his lower lip, and the stubborn set of his jaw suggested that this wasn't working out the way Scott had hoped.

Runyan dropped into a chair across the table and rolled a smoke. He said, "George Vance stopped on his way home and told us about Alec Schmidt being here. Mighty smart, that old boy. I've never met him, but I'd heard a lot about him before Bengogh showed up with the company herd."

"He's a cold-blooded fish," Scott said.

"Cold-blooded but smart," Runyan said. "You and Patsy and Sally hollered so much about trouble that I was beginning to think I'd have some. Now I don't figure I will. Alec's too smart. I know how he operates."

So Runyan had made up his mind. Scott said, "You won't try driving across company range, then?"

Runyan shrugged. "Not now. Time settles everything, Travis. I figure to give it a chance."

Sally was standing with her back to the stove, her arms folded across her breasts. She said coldly, "You're just like you were when you were little, Jay. You'd rather have your own way than be right. I guess you'll never change."

"I'll change him," Patsy said.

"You've got something to learn about your future husband," Sally said. "Jay, even if you won't have anything to do with the drive, you can do something for Scott and his friends."

He looked at her through a cloud of cigarette smoke. "What?"

"They want to live here and have their own outfit. You can help them get a start."

"Why, sure," Runyan said. "I'll do that, seeing as you're my sister."

Scott had started to reach for his coffee cup. Now he dropped his hand to the table as he said curtly, "We'll make our own way. We ain't asking for no handouts."

Sally flushed, but she held her temper. "I'm being practical, Jay, for your sake as well as the others. We'll need Scott and his friends when trouble comes, and it will come as soon as Schmidt goes back to San Francisco."

"We'll keep 'em in the valley," Runyan said tolerantly. "We can use good men, trouble or no trouble."

"I've got a hunch about Bengogh." Scott lifted his coffee cup and drank, studying Runyan's blocky face over the rim of his cup. The man was stubborn; but he wasn't stupid, and Vance had said he was not a coward. "Figuring from my hunch, I sort o' changed my notion about how to do this job. Sooner or later you and the rest of 'em will have to make that drive. How big a herd will it be?"

"Oh, maybe fifteen hundred. Why?"

"I was wondering about the crew. Vance will go, but four of us ain't enough. You reckon we can get two or three more?"

"Sure." Runyan shrugged. "When the time comes."

"The time's here," Sally said bitterly. "Why can't you see that, Jay?"

"Maybe it ain't." Scott reached for a biscuit. "If my hunch is right it'll be better to play this out for a few weeks. Sally's letter may fetch the governor into this deal."

"I've said all the time there ain't no hurry," Runyan said, "but I won't count on the governor stepping in. George told us what Schmidt said about paying taxes and all, and I figure he's right. A man like him always has political connections."

Patsy was standing behind Runyan. She had been watching Scott closely. Now she asked, "Just what is this hunch you're talking about?"

Scott looked up from his plate. "I couldn't put my hands on nothing, but I've been thinking on it all afternoon. I've got a notion there's something between Schmidt and Bengogh that ain't just right. Schmidt said he done his best to get along with his neighbors. Well, Bengogh hasn't even tried to get along, so it struck me that maybe he'd lost his job."

Runyan nodded. "Might work that way."

"When you do make the drive," Scott said, "we'd like to have a job."

Someone was riding in, and Runyan rose. "No reason why you can't have it." He moved toward the living-room door and stopped, looking at Scott. "How are you three going to make a living till you get your outfit going?"

"One of us will run the ranch, and the other two work. Must be some jobs around."

"The mines around Canyon City," Patsy said.

Runyan nodded. "They're always needing some freighters. Might get on driving stage. Plenty of work, all right." And he left the room.

Scott finished eating and leaned back to smoke a cigarette as the girls cleared the table and brought the pies out of the pantry.

"We'd better start the coffee," Patsy said. "We'll need ten gallons before they get done with this palaver."

Sally nodded, her face bleak. Scott, watching her, sensed that she was angry about something; but whether it was because he had gone with Vance to the company ranch, or whether she had been unable to convince her brother that he should challenge Bengogh, was a question.

He finished his cigarette, thinking that twice today he had risked his life. He had no regrets, for his motive had been selfish enough, and when a man played for high stakes he had to accept whatever personal risk was involved. Still, Runyan and his neighbors were the ones who stood to make the biggest profit, and they should be willing to share the risk. From the way Runyan talked, he wasn't willing to risk anything.

Someone had come into the front room with Runyan, and Scott rose, his gaze on Sally, who had just set two pies on the table. He said, "Looks like you did some work today."

"Mostly Patsy."

"What kind are they?"

"Dried-apple and peach." She looked at him, her slender back arrow-straight, the contrary lock of hair dangling across her forehead. She brushed it back, and then said impulsively, "You can't put this off, Scott. I don't understand you."

"Your brother was right about time being the answer; but, either way, it's a long-odds gamble. Just seemed to me that the chances are a little better if we wait."

"No," Sally breathed. "You're wrong. If you wait you'll lose all the advantage you have now."

Runyan called from the living-room, "Travis!"

"We'll see," Scott said, and left the kitchen.

George Vance and Hank Nolan were with Runyan in the living-room, and as Scott came in a dozen ranchers fled through the front door and were introduced to him. He sat down on a bench beside Vance, who leaned toward him and said in a low tone, "When I stopped here this afternoon, I think Jay was ready to take a crack at Bengogh; but I made the mistake of telling him Schmidt was here, and he began backing off."

"It's all right," Scott said. "I'd have told him if you hadn't."

Yates and Bemis came in and sat down beside Scott, Bemis asking, "Time to start the ball, ain't it, Vance?"

"They're all here," Vance said. "Dunno what Jay's waiting for."

"Find out," Bemis said impatiently.

Vance started to get up and sat back again, his face troubled. "Don't think I'd better open my mug. My luck with this bunch has been all bad."

Bemis began to fidget. Scott, looking around the room, did not see anyone except Runyan who showed any promise of leadership. The steady beat of talk came to him, about grass, the need of rain, the price of beef that was better than it had been for years, a horse trade a couple of them had just made. It was the kind of talk he had heard in Nebraska when cowmen got together, but there was a difference. Bengogh's shadow lay upon the room.

This casual talk could go on for hours because all

the ranchers including Jay Runyan were afraid to face the issue which sooner or later must be met. Now, looking at Nolan's wrinkled, worried face, Scott decided he had been wrong in saying that time might be the answer. Sally was right. If they waited they lost their advantage. Schmidt had blandly said the road was not closed. This, then, was the time to make the test while Schmidt was still in the valley.

Scott had been caught in a trap of indecision, thinking that the smart way would be to wait for Bengogh's mistake. Now he made up his mind, or rather Sally had made it up for him. She knew these men, she knew her brother; and, while she hadn't said it in so many words, she had certainly indicated that if they didn't fight now they would go on waiting.

Bemis said, "I'm gonna find out what's holding this deal up."

"Wait," Scott said. "I'll ask Runyan." He rose and crossed the room to Runyan. "Jay, ain't it time we got at it?"

Runyan looked up. "Your move, Travis."

Nolan, beside him, said quietly, "No, Jay. It's yours. If you won't I will."

Runyan stared at the banker. "How'd you get in this game?"

"I've been in it from the day Bengogh evicted everybody from the lake."

The talk had died. For a tense moment there was this uneasy silence, Runyan and Nolan glaring at each other, neither willing to make the start that somebody had to make. Sally, in the kitchen doorway, said, "Must be a Quaker meeting."

Somebody snickered nervously, and Vance said, "Reckon I got in the wrong meetinghouse. I ain't a Quaker."

"Neither am I," Sally said, "so I'll talk since

nobody else wants to. You've all met Scott Travis and his two friends. You've heard that Scott licked Wick Tally in a fist fight, and that he gunned Jimmy Kane down today. He's a stranger, and that's an advantage because he hasn't been intimidated by Bengogh as the rest of us have."

"Now, Sally—" Runyan began.

"Shut up, Jay. All you can say is wait. Well, we've waited, and look at what it got us. Hank, I think you know better than anyone else what will happen if we keep on waiting."

Nolan nodded. "I know, all right. It's mighty damned simple, boys. All of you but Jay owe me money. Your notes are due this fall. Sure, your cattle are worth more than you owe me, but I can't meet my obligations with steers. I've got to have money, cash money, and you can't give it to me unless you get a herd through to Winnemucca."

"That's where we come in," Scott said. "Me and Bemis and Yates have done plenty of driving. Jay says you'll have a herd of about fifteen hundred head. How long will it take to gather that herd?"

"A month," a man said. "But maybe you don't know what'll happen when we start across Bengogh's range?"

"We know," Scott said curtly. "George, will you go?"

"You're damned right," Vance said, "and I'm taking my Winchester along."

"I'll go," Patsy said.

Runyan jumped up. "Patsy, you stay out—"

"I'm in," she said defiantly. "There's just one thing I want to do besides marry you, and that's to get Bengogh. Maybe you've forgotten, but I'm remembering how my father died."

"And I'll go," Sally said. "You've got six trail hands, Scott. That enough?"

Scott grinned. "That'll do. All right, here's our

deal. We want one heifer from each of you for every ten steers we drive to the railroad, and we'll pick the heifers." He looked around the circle of men. "Is it a deal?"

Runyan looked as if he were about to choke. The rest glanced at one another uneasily, saying nothing, and Scott knew how it was. If Runyan said it was a deal the rest would follow; but Runyan maintained a stubborn silence.

Bemis got up. "If an outfit like this can be showed up by a couple of girls, why, hell, we'd best fork our horses and ride."

"Don't hurry this," Nolan said. "I want these boys to know how it stands. I've got to take up those notes on their due dates. If you can't pay I'll take your steers, and these men will drive them to Winnemucca for me."

"I've got fifty head," Vance said. "I'll start gathering 'em tomorrow. I ain't waiting for you to grab my cattle, Hank."

"I'm in," a lanky man said. "I've got about eighty head, I reckon."

Another man beside him nodded. "Count me in. I've got better'n a hundred four-year-olds."

"You gonna help on the drive?" Runyan demanded.

The lanky man nodded. "If two girls can go I reckon I can." He looked at Scott. "Just one thing bothers me. We don't know you boys. What's gonna keep you from taking the money and lighting a shuck out of Winnemucca?"

Scott turned and met his gaze. He said in a tight, brittle voice, "Not a damned thing."

The man shifted uneasily, licked his lips, and looked at Nolan. "Hank, don't look like this is the answer."

"You knuckle-headed idiot," Nolan shouted. "Just be sure you can meet your note the day it's due. Maybe you've got the right answer, but it had better jingle when you bring it to the bank."

It hung that way for a moment, Sally glaring at Runyan, who still refused to say the word that would change the inertia which gripped the crowd; then a man sitting beside the door said, "Somebody's coming."

Runyan jumped up and walked to the door. "Busting the breeze, too. Something's happened."

He went outside, the others streaming behind him. Scott waited for Sally, and when she came toward him he said, "You were right about putting this off, but it don't look like it'll go. Holding back gets to be a habit."

She gave him a tight smile. "A habit can be broken."

Patsy, standing beside her, said, "I don't know why I ever told that Jay I'd marry him. Now I've got to tell him different."

The rider had pulled up in the yard. He called, "Travis around?"

"Hibbard," Patsy breathed as if she could not believe it. "What would fetch him up here?"

Scott went out on the porch. He said, "I'm here."

Hibbard had dismounted outside the pool of lamplight that fell across the yard from the open door. Now he pushed through the crowd and faced Scott, a cocked gun in his hand. He said, "Drop your gun belt, Travis. I'm arresting you for the murder of Alec Schmidt."

Chapter 17: Arrest

FOR A MOMENT THEY STOOD THERE LIKE FIGURES OF A tableau, the silence ribboning out. Hibbard stood spread-legged, his gun lined on Scott, his gaunt face filled with a crazy, reckless determination. He had steeled himself to do this job, Scott thought, but he was dangerous, for a weak man's courage is always questionable. The slightest move on Scott's part would bring death.

Runyan made a slow turn to face Scott. He said, "You took a pretty strong measure to settle our trouble."

"I didn't kill him," Scott said, watching Hibbard.

"It ain't for me to say whether you did or not," Hibbard said. "Tally and Delazon say they'll swear in court that they saw you gun him down. They chased you, and you outran 'em. They took the body to the ranch, and then the crew brought it to town."

"Who do you reckon they're lying for?" Scott asked.

"If they're lying it's for Bengogh; but I don't know they're lying. That's for a jury to decide."

Sally was standing beside Scott now. She cried, "Frank, you're such a fool. Can't you see why Bengogh is trying to put this on Scott?"

"I can think of a reason or two," Hibbard said; "but somebody shot him. I saw the body, and, with Tally and Delazon saying Travis done it, I've got to take him in."

"Was it a fight?" Runyan asked. "I mean, did Schmidt have a gun?"

"No. Tally said he never carried a gun. That makes it murder."

"Where was I supposed to be? Just riding around hunting for Schmidt?" Scott asked.

"According to Tally, you were hiding in a gulch. There's one out there, all right, deep enough to hide a horse and rider. Tally says they didn't see you till you rode out of that gulch, plugged the old man, and then you headed north hell for leather."

"How would I know that gulch was there?"

"You might have seen it when you was with Vance this afternoon, or somebody might have told you." Hibbard's gaze swung briefly to Sally and back to Travis. "I won't ask you again to drop your gun belt."

Sally stepped down from the porch. "Frank, you can't do this. You're playing Bengogh's game for him. Can't you understand that?"

"Sure, you'd think that; but I've got my duty, and I'm aiming to do it."

She was close to him now. "Frank, can you ever respect yourself again if you do Bengogh's dirty chores for him?"

"I've got my duty—"

She jumped at him and grabbed Hibbard's gun arm. The hammer dropped, the explosion beating against Scott's ears as he came off the porch in a diving lunge. The bullet had missed him by inches. Hibbard threw Sally away from him and jerked the gun free; then Scott had his arm and twisted it until he cried out in pain and dropped the Colt. Runyan grabbed Hibbard by the shoulder from behind, jerked him around, hit him in the face, and knocked him down.

"You locoed fool!" he shouted with a depth of

violence Scott did not know he was capable of showing. "You might have killed Sally."

Someone yelled, "Let's get a rope. He's been Bengogh's man ever since we voted him into office."

Hibbard sat up, feeling of the side of his face where Runyan had hit him. "I came here to do my duty," he said in a trembling voice. "Now you're making outlaws out of yourselves, and for a drifter who don't mean a thing to any of you."

Bemis and Yates crowded up. Bemis said darkly, "He means something to us. We ain't letting you take him to town for Bengogh to hang. Let's ride, Scott."

"No." Scott glanced at Sally. From the expression on her face, he knew that he meant something to her, and he couldn't leave. "I'll go with you, Hibbard, but I'm keeping my gun."

"You can't, Scott." Sally came to him, gripping his arms frantically as if trying to make her fingers as well as her voice convince him that he couldn't go with Hibbard. "They'll hang you. Maybe Bengogh killed Schmidt himself. Or Tally. But they're trying to get you out of the way. Don't you see?"

"I see that; but Hibbard's right about everybody making outlaws out of themselves. I can't let that happen." He looked at the sheriff, who was on his feet now, still rubbing his face. "Is Bengogh's crew in town?"

"Yeah, they're in the saloon," Hibbard said sullenly. "Purty hot under the collar, too. They liked Schmidt. Most of 'em have worked for him for years."

"Hibbard, I might have believed Travis killed him except for one thing," Runyan said slowly. "He ain't the kind who'd ride out of a gulch and shoot an unarmed man."

"How the hell do you know that?"

"I know a man when I see one," Runyan answered. "I'll see that Travis stays here. He'll be in town for trial when he's needed. You've got my word for that."

"Won't do," Hibbard cried. "I've got to take him to jail. If you won't let him go I'll deputize Bengogh's crew, and we'll come and get him. You'll have hell to pay then."

"I'm going with you," Scott said. "There's been enough killing today."

Sally still held to his arms, looking up at him, and the lamplight from the house fell upon her face. He gave her a wry smile, wanting to tell her that he loved her, that he would see this through to the finish because of her, but this was not the time. He knew what he had to do, and if he did not come back to her he did not want her to be bound in any way to the memory of a dead man.

"Scott, Scott!" she breathed. "Is this the way it will always be, just fighting?"

"No, not after tonight."

He pulled free from her hands and, stooping, picked up Hibbard's gun and slipped it under his waistband. When he straightened up Bemis and Yates stood in front of him, their faces dark with bitterness.

"We've played along with you, Scott," Bemis said, "on a deal that looked like a damned-fool proposition from the start. If you go with Hibbard we're done with you."

"You bet we are," Yates added. "We're riding over the hill tonight."

"No, you ain't," Scott said. "I'll need you before morning. Jay, I'd like a fresh horse. My black is pretty well played out."

"Sure," Runyan said, and turned toward the corral.

Patsy cried, "Jay, you're making a mistake you'll always regret if you let him go."

"He's a stubborn man." Runyan looked back at her. "A real stubborn man. Maybe you can change his mind."

Runyan went on, Scott falling into step beside him, while the rest stared after them. Scott, glancing back, saw that Sally had run into the house, her head bowed. Doubts crowded into his mind, and again he wondered if a man was ever sure what was the right thing to do at a time like this. Then he smothered the doubts as he thought of Bengogh. A man had to play the cards that fell to him, and he had to play them the way he saw it, not the way someone else would play the same hand.

Runyan stepped into the barn for a lantern, lighted it, and brought it to the corral gate. He hung it on a nail, saying, "I've got a sorrel that's fresh. Might pitch a time or two, but, once you get him ironed out, he'll go a long ways."

Waiting at the gate until Runyan brought the horse, Scott lifted the saddle to the animal's back and tightened the cinch. Then he said, "Jay, I've got a notion about this."

"Figured you did," Runyan said.

"You told me you didn't want to be a leader; but you're gonna be tonight, whether you like it or not."

"Looks like it. What do you want me to do?"

"I told you I had a hunch about there being something between Schmidt and Bengogh. This makes it look like I was right. I figure Bengogh shot Schmidt."

"Why?" Runyan demanded. "Hell, he had a good job. No sense in killing his boss."

"I don't know why, but I aim to find out. All your trouble goes back to Bengogh. When we get him your trouble's finished."

He had expected Runyan to say he had no trouble with Bengogh, but Runyan surprised him. "One thing's sure; I won't have no peace with Patsy till Bengogh's finished. But I don't savvy why you—"

"Sally," Scott said, "and that outfit I'm bound to own. I've wasted a lot of years, Jay. Well, I'm staying here, so I figure I've got a stake in this valley, too. I don't expect this to make sense to you; but, damn it, I've got something inside me that says this is what I want. I want it bad enough to fight for it."

"Maybe I understand." Runyan held out his hand. "Sally feels the same way about you. Good luck, boy."

Scott grasped the hand. "Thanks. I just want you to do one thing. Come along half an hour behind me, and keep Bengogh's crew in the saloon."

"We'll do it," Runyan said.

Scott stepped into the saddle and let the sorrel buck. By the time he was across the yard the horse had settled down. He called, "Let's ride, Hibbard."

No one said anything as Hibbard mounted and joined him. When they rode away, the men in front of the house stared after them, a vague, motionless knot in the fringe of lamplight. A thin moon was showing above the eastern rimrock, and the sky was clear and sparkling with the cold, distant brilliance of the stars.

For a time Hibbard held a sullen silence. Then they reached the road that led into Piute, and he burst out, "What's this going to buy you, Travis, taking me in instead of me taking you in?"

"Quite a bit, if my scheme works." Scott hesitated, then forced himself to say one thing that he felt must be said. "Patsy told me you and Sally are engaged."

"Not any more," Hibbard said bitterly. "I thought she'd told you."

"Told me what?"

"She broke it off today. On account of you, I reckon."

Scott could not trust his voice for a moment. Then he said, "I was aiming to tell you I'm in love with her. If I live I'll ask her to marry me."

"I ain't in your way. But I reckon your coming didn't change anything. We didn't belong to each other. I've known it a long time, but I just kept hoping. You'd better make her happy, Travis, or, so help me, I'll cut your heart out."

Scott stared at the man's gaunt face in the thin light, sensing the unhappiness and frustration that was in him, and sensing, too, that the pressure of these last hours had hardened the iron in him—iron that he probably had not realized he possessed. Scott had seen it happen to other men, and in a way it was what had happened to him.

"I'll do my damnedest," Scott said.

Hibbard spoke as if he hadn't heard. "Don't make sense—not when you think about it—a stranger riding in and changing everything in a few hours; but it happened just the same. You turned this valley inside out the minute you hit Piute."

They rode in silence again, and presently the light of Piute showed ahead of them. Scott said, "I want to make a deal with you, Hibbard. If it don't pan out I'll give you my gun and yours, too."

"I can't make a deal with you," Hibbard said stubbornly. "I'm the sheriff, and you're my prisoner."

"Is it on account of Sally?"

"No, God damn it! I'd have lost her anyway." The sheriff paused, and then burst out, "I've never been any good, Travis. Not the way folks judge a man in this country. I told Sally I was afraid to live, and that's the truth. Been trying to hang on to something I wasn't man enough to hold. She wanted me to leave the country before this happened, but I couldn't do it—I just couldn't do it."

Scott understood then. Frank Hibbard had been fighting his own weakness all this time; and what Patsy had said about him must have been the general opinion. Now, after the break with Sally, the sheriff was determined to prove himself. That was the reason he had come after Scott.

"It took guts to arrest me. A lot of guts, with you knowing how the odds stood."

Hibbard sucked in a long breath. "More'n I thought I had."

"I figure it ain't what a man's been in the past," Scott went on. "It's what he's gonna be in the future. I'm a lot like you, Hibbard. I came to this valley to rob the bank, but I didn't. Instead I got hold of something that's worth doing."

"Tally told me about the bank deal. Claims he got it from Delazon."

"You didn't tell Sally."

"I didn't believe it. Just hearsay anyhow."

"Might have turned Sally against me."

"I thought of that," Hibbard said sourly, "but I didn't know it was true. Hell! You can't go around believing everything somebody like Wick Tally says."

"You're square," Scott said.

"I try to be." Hibbard turned to stare at him, wanting his approval, wanting to be believed. "God knows I try to be."

They had reached the edge of town, and Main Street lay before them, a wide strip of dust covered by alternate patches of lamplight and darkness. Scott reined up, "Will you listen to me, Hibbard?"

Hibbard stopped. "You're going to jail."

"Not yet. I want to make that deal. If you won't listen, I'll have to tackle it alone."

Hibbard sat his saddle as if he were frozen there.

Then he said sullenly. "You've got me hipped. Speak your piece."

"I figure Bengogh killed Schmidt, and he's framing me. If we can get him alone we'll get the truth out of him."

"He wouldn't have any reason to kill Schmidt."

"I think he has, but I don't know what it is. You see, he's been pretty cute. You went after me, and his crew is waiting here in town. One of two things was bound to happen. You'd bring me in and his crew would lynch me, or—"

"I wouldn't let 'em," Hibbard broke in.

"Could you save my neck by yourself against a bunch that was bound to square up for Schmidt?"

Hibbard hesitated; then he said honestly, "No, I couldn't."

"All right. If you didn't bring me in, the chances were I'd kill you, the way Bengogh looks at it. Or Runyan and the rest would have kept you from arresting me like they were gonna do, and then you'd have come for the crew like you said you would. That would make me bullet bait, and maybe get half the little ranchers killed, which is what Bengogh wants. It'd put the law on his side to boot."

For a long moment Hibbard was silent. Scott could not tell what was going through his mind, torn between his habitual sense of failure and his new, fanatical resolve to do his duty and gain the respect he had failed to receive through the years he had carried the star.

Without a gun Hibbard was helpless, and that perhaps decided him. He said, "Well, it makes sense. But I don't see what you're driving at."

"I want you to go with me to the company ranch and hear what Bengogh has to say; but before we do that we'd better sneak into town and see what the crew has been saying. I want to know if they're all here. Bengogh may have been smart enough to pull some of the boys back to the ranch."

"We can't fight a dozen men," Hibbard said. "You're loco."

"I don't want to fight 'em. Is there anybody we can trust who wouldn't be suspected of working with me?"

"The sawbones."

"Would he be in his office?"

"Probably."

"Can we get into the back of his office without being seen?"

Hibbard hesitated, weighing the possibilities. "I think so. It's pretty dark."

"Go ahead," Scott said. "I'll follow."

Hibbard reined his horse off the road and made a wide half-circle through the grass at the edge of town. Scott kept a few feet behind, listening for any sound that might indicate they had been seen. This was a long-odds gamble; a slip now would bring the wolf pack down on him, and he would never live to get at Bengogh.

Chapter 18: The String Ravels Out

THE TOWN WAS OMINOUSLY SILENT, THE WINDOWS OF most of the dwellings dark. Hibbard was north of the middle of Main Street when he made his turn, reined up, and dismounted. "Be less racket if we walk in," he said.

Scott hesitated, uneasy. He didn't want to be caught this far from his horse, but Hibbard was probably right. If any of Bengogh's men were on the street and heard horses coming in, there would be hell to pay. He stepped down and, leaving the sorrel ground-hitched, followed through the tall weeds of a vacant lot to the back door of the doctor's office.

Hibbard tapped lightly, and tried the knob when there was no response. The door was locked.

Scott asked, "Does he live here?"

"Yeah. He's got his bed and stove in the back room. Chances are, he's in the front but I hate like hell to go around."

Scott put his face to a window and peered through it. He could see a thin line of light around a door at the far end of the room. "Try again, Hibbard. He's in there."

Hibbard knocked louder, and when nothing happened, he began to pound, the door shaking under his fist. Light flooded the back room, and heavy steps crossed to the door. The doctor unlocked and opened it, saying in a furious voice, "My office is in the front. If you want—"

"Move back," Scott said, "so that lamp you're holding don't light up the whole alley."

The doctor peered into the darkness, the lamp held high. Then he recognized them, blew the lamp out, and put it down on the table. "Come in."

Scott stepped into the room, followed by Hibbard, who closed the door. The doctor pulled the blinds and lighted the lamp again, cursing the hot chimney. He made a slow turn, looking at Hibbard and then at Scott, frankly puzzled.

"I didn't kill Schmidt," Scott said. "I think Bengogh did, and we're going to the company ranch to find out."

The doctor rubbed a hand across his neck, turning to Hibbard. "This is the damnedest thing I ever saw. Are you his prisoner, sheriff?"

Red-faced, Hibbard said, "Something like that."

"No, he ain't," Scott said sharply. "I made a deal. If I don't get nothing out of Bengogh, I promised to give him my gun and he'll lock me up. He's going along to hear Bengogh put a rope on his own neck."

"You're being childish. Bengogh will never talk. Anyhow, his crew is in town. If they spot you, they'll put a rope on your neck."

Scott gave a tight grin. "Nothing like going whole hog, doc. Hibbard said you could be trusted. Today you got off some talk about there being different kinds of men, each of you doing what you could. All right, how about you?"

The doctor sat down, suddenly as if his knees had given out and could no longer hold him. "I want things in this valley changed as bad as the next man, but if you think I'm going to take a gun—"

"No," Scott broke in. "We don't have a hell of a lot of time. I want to know what the crew aims to do, and if all of 'em are in town. Can you find out for us without letting on we're here?"

"Maybe." The doctor scratched his fat nose, glancing at Hibbard. "So you don't think Travis here killed Schmidt?"

"Dunno," the sheriff said. "I didn't have much choice. They were fixing to hang me out there at the Triangle R. This is Travis's idea."

The medico's eyes swung back to Scott. "How do you know Bengogh did it?"

"In the first place, I know I didn't. In the second place, I can't think of anybody else who would have. It takes a certain kind of man to plug a fellow the way Schmidt was, him not packing a gun. I figure Bengogh is that kind."

The doctor considered this a minute, then he nodded. "Yeah, I think he would be. Well, you'd be doing a big thing for this valley if you nailed Marvin Bengogh. Stay here. I won't be gone long."

He went out through the front, leaving the lamp on the table. Scott stood at the side of the door leading into the office, and waited, the minutes dragging out. He could be sold out, but he was gambling on what Hibbard had said about the doctor and on his own judgment of the man. Although he was sure of that judgment, his nerves tightened with the passing minutes until he thought he could not stand it.

Then the front door opened, and he heard the doctor's voice. "It won't take you more'n a minute, Chubby. Come on back. There's something funny about those bullet holes. Looks like his killer was standing mighty damned close."

Scott motioned for Hibbard to remain where he could not be seen from the office. The doctor walked in, saying over his shoulder, "I figure this will be quite a surprise, Chubby."

A fat buckaroo came into the room; he saw Hibbard and stiffened. "You get Travis?"

"Behind you," Hibbard said.

Chubby swung around and was gripped by terror. Then he began to curse and grabbed his gun. He had it half lifted from leather when Scott hit him on the side of the head, knocking him back against the wall, and caught his wrist, twisting it violently. He cried out in pain and dropped the gun.

Scott kicked it across the room. "What'd you bring him in for, doc?"

"He's rodding the crew," the medico answered. "I've got a storeroom where I'll keep him while you and Frank do your chore. I figured I'd pin the crew here so you wouldn't have them on your neck."

"Jay Runyan is bringing his bunch in," Scott said. "They'll hold 'em."

"I didn't know that. There wasn't time anyhow. They were getting ready to go after you."

"You're damned right." Chubby stood with his back to the wall, a hand touching the side of his face where Scott had hit him. "We figured you'd had time to plug Hibbard, and you'd be on the run. We're gonna string you up, boy."

"Why didn't you come after me in the first place?" Scott asked.

"Bengogh's idea," Chubby said sullenly. "He wanted the law on our side; and if you'd plugged Hibbard, which Bengogh seemed to be sure you'd do, everybody would be hunting you."

Scott nodded at the sheriff. "I guessed right."

"Looks like it," Hibbard agreed. "Suppose I'd locked him up."

"We'd have hung him," Chubby answered sullenly. "We ain't waiting on what you call the law, not when it's Alec Schmidt who got beefed."

"All the crew in the saloon?" Scott asked.

"The regular hands." Chubby was still sullen. "Tally and Delazon went back to the ranch."

This was what Scott wanted to know. "Lock him up, doc. We'll be riding."

"I didn't know Delazon was hooked up with Bengogh," the doctor said. "He's just a cattle buyer—"

"That's a long yarn." Scott picked up Chubby's gun and gave it to the doctor. "Lock the fat boy up. If you let him get away, we're finished."

"I'll keep him." The doctor opened a side door and motioned for Chubby to go through it. "Or, if I don't, I'll kill him."

Scott waited until the door was locked on the cursing buckaroo. "Any windows in that room?"

"No windows. Just a storeroom, and it's got solid walls. He won't kick his way out."

Scott blew out the lamp. "Light it as soon as we're out." And he slid through the back door, Hibbard following.

They waited for a moment, Scott thinking he would hear Runyan and his men, but there was no sound of incoming horses. They went back across the weedy lot and, mounting, circled the town and hit the road to the company ranch.

They kept a steady, ground-eating pace, the lights of Piute dying behind them. Neither man had any inclination to talk. So far, Scott felt, it had worked out well. What lay ahead was another matter. He had no faith in Hibbard when the chips were down, and he wondered what was in the man's mind. He was not even sure the sheriff could be trusted, but there was no choice.

Surprise was the one element which might break Bengogh. He could wait for Runyan, and could take Bemis and Yates along; but there was no telling how soon they would be in town, or even whether they would come at all. To hold the advantage of surprise, he must use the margin of time he held.

The odds were not too long. Scott discounted Delazon. Wick Tally was the dangerous man. But there was the chance that he could get into the house without Tally's knowledge. Bengogh had no reason to think his plan had failed, and would probably not be on guard.

Scott felt strongly that everything, even his life, would be won or lost tonight. Bengogh must have had a motive for murdering Schmidt. He had to find out what it was; he had to either get a confession from Bengogh or find proof of his guilt. Killing him wasn't enough.

Scott thought about Ellen Schmidt, who would undoubtedly inherit her husband's property. However the company was organized, Schmidt certainly controlled it. The question was, what would happen after Mrs. Schmidt returned to San Francisco? She might send somebody north to run the company ranch the same way Bengogh had. In that case, nothing would be gained. But that bridge could be crossed later. Bengogh was the immediate problem.

The ranch house was a tiny pin point of lamp-light ahead of them in the pressing darkness; it grew steadily larger, and within the hour Scott and Hibbard reached the yard. They had pulled their horses down to a walk, hoofs making only a whisper of sound in the thick matting of grass, and now they reined up some distance from the patches of light that fell through the living-room windows and the open front door.

"How are we playing this?" Hibbard asked, unable to disguise his uneasiness.

"We'll circle the light," Scott answered, "and Injun up to the front door. I'm handling Bengogh. You keep Delazon and Tally off my neck."

They dismounted, leaving the reins trailing. Hibbard said, "You gonna give me my gun?"

Scott handed it over. "Don't make no racket. That's our only chance."

"A damned slim one," Hibbard muttered.

They made a wide circle of the lighted area, moving swiftly and silently, and reached the dark east side of the house. Crouching, they moved around the corner and crossed the porch to the front door, keeping under a window so that there would be no moving shadow to give their presence away. They stopped beside the door, hugging the wall.

Scott put a hand out to keep Hibbard behind him, whispering, "We'll wait," and drew his gun.

The minutes dragged by with no sound from the interior of the house. Scott still was not sure the sheriff would not shove his gun into his back and yell for Tally and Delazon; but there was nothing to do now but trust him. One element encouraged Scott; Hibbard had lost Sally but still wanted her approval, wanted to show her that at the finish he had a man's courage; and he could not do that by going over to Bengogh's side.

Presently Hibbard breathed, "We can't sit here all night. I've got a cramp in my leg."

"Stand up," Scott whispered "I don't savvy this. Oughtta be talk—someone moving around—anything."

"Maybe Bengogh ain't here."

"Nowhere for him to go unless he's leaving the country, and that wouldn't look good."

"Then they're expecting callers, and we'll walk into some hot lead when we go through that door."

"Yeah. I was thinking that."

"We could go around to the back."

"You know the layout?"

"No."

"Then we've got to do it this way. We'd just make a lot of racket if we tried the back."

Hibbard was on his feet, a board on the porch floor squealing under him. He swore softly. "If anybody's in that living-room they've heard us by now."

"Might bring 'em out."

Again they were silent, and time dragged out while tension worked on Scott. He had expected Bengogh and Mrs. Schmidt to be in the living-room; he had thought he would hear their talk. It seemed unlikely they would have gone to bed after what had happened.

Now the silence worried him. He had not counted on this. He wanted to get his gun on Bengogh, to make the man break under the threat of death. Now he was caught. The silence was unnatural. Bengogh must be in his room, or in the office where he would be safe. Probably Tally and Delazon were inside with their guns in their hands. If they were, Scott and Hibbard would be cut down the instant they appeared in the lamplight.

Scott felt Hibbard's hand on his shoulder, heard him whisper, "Somebody's coming."

Scott caught it then, the thunder of hoofs sweeping across the grass from the north. "More'n one rider," he breathed, and thought that it must be the crew. The doctor had let Chubby escape.

"The crew," Hibbard said in a low, frantic voice. "We're in a squeeze now, Travis. A hell of an idea you had!"

For an instant Scott thought Hibbard was going to make a run for it; but the man didn't move. The drum of hoofs was clearer now, coming in on the night breeze. A large party, maybe a dozen men. Hibbard was right about their being caught in a squeeze. It might be suicide to lunge through the door, but there was the possibility that Tally and Delazon were outside. If that was true it would be as dangerous to try to get back to the horses.

For a moment Scott was caught in a trap of indecision. He felt as if his stomach had dropped a foot; he had the rump-tingling feeling of the knowledge that, whichever way he jumped, he was asking for a bullet. Then he made up his mind. No sense in waiting here and being trapped with Bengogh's crew moving in.

"We're going through the door. Might have a chance inside."

Before Scott could move he heard footsteps pound toward the house, and Delazon's big voice. "Bengogh! Somebody's coming. Bengogh, you hear?"

Scott made out his great bulk in the fringe of light. He called, "Throw down your gun, Delazon."

Panic must have seized the big man, for he let out a squall and threw a shot at the spot where he judged Scott to be standing. The bullet came close, slapping into the wall between the two; then Scott pulled the trigger and Delazon spilled forward, his hand thrown out. He fell on his belly, twitched, and lay still.

Time had run out. A feeling of failure rushed through Scott. He had hoped to have a few minutes with Bengogh; but now it was a question of survival, and there seemed to be little chance of that. He dived through the door and put his back to the wall.

For an instant he had been silhouetted against the lamplight; but there was no gunfire. His eyes swept the big room. No one was in sight. He glimpsed Hibbard, who had lunged into the room; he took a step toward the office, thinking Bengogh must be there, and then he heard a woman scream—a long, sustained sound, shrill and high and terrifying.

"Upstairs," Hibbard bawled.

Scott wheeled; at the head of the stairs Bengogh was struggling with Mrs. Schmidt, her blouse torn, her blond hair cascading down her back. Scott raised his gun instinctively. Hibbard screamed frantically, "No, Travis, you'll hit her."

Scott held his fire. For a moment at least Mrs. Schmidt was keeping Bengogh from using the long-barreled Colt he had in his hand. Then he felt something like a great hammer blow in the back that knocked him flat on his face, the sound of the shot very loud.

Other shots, a man's high yell of agony, and then Bengogh came hurtling down the stairs, trying to catch himself and failing. Scott held to his gun and raised himself on his hands and knees as Bengogh hit the floor in front of him.

Bengogh jumped to his feet. He had lost his Colt, but was tugging a derringer out of his coat pocket. He had been shaken by the fall and was slow. The amiable expression with which he habitually masked his feelings was stripped from a face contorted by terror. Mrs. Schmidt, at the head of the stairs, was still screaming.

These few seconds seemed like an eternity to

Scott. More shots were thundering behind him; but whether they were from Hibbard's gun or someone else's he did not know. He watched Bengogh's face as a man might watch a buzzing rattlesnake; he saw the derringer swing out from Bengogh's pocket, with a strange feeling as if he were a detached spectator.

Suddenly he realized that his own gun was firing. He felt the solid buck of it in his hand; he saw the up-drifting balloon of smoke. Bengogh bent forward, his chin tipping down against his chest; then every joint seemed to break at once, and he went down.

Scott's arms and knees gave under him, and he went flat on his face. Mrs. Schmidt's screams still came shrilly to him, but they seemed distant. He heard other voices, Jay Runyan's great shout, and Hibbard yelling, "I got Tally. You hear? I got Wick Tally."

People crowded into the room. Scott had the crazy sensation that he was seeing each person twice. That was queer. The thought nudged him that a man couldn't see anyone twice at the same time. Then Sally was on the floor, cradling his head in her lap and crying unabashedly. She kept saying, "You can't die, darling, you can't die!" And Ed Bemis's voice, "I'll get the doc."

Mrs. Schmidt was still screaming. Runyan said, "Go upstairs to the crazy woman, Patsy." And Hibbard again: "I got Tally, Jay. You hear me?" A lot of people. The room was jammed with them. A lot of voices, running together and garbled, with only Sally's coming clearly to Scott. Then he seemed to be falling without anything holding him, falling into nothingness, and Sally's voice no longer came to him.

Scott's sense of time played tricks on him. Hours became days, and days weeks, all flowing out into a continuous stream that was unmarked. Sally was often with him; the doctor, at times. Hank Nolan and Jay Runyan. Shorty Yates and Ed Bemis. And there were other moments when he was alone and a black vulture sat on a bedpost watching him with malicious satisfaction. The vulture had the face of Marvin Bengogh.

Later—he had no idea how much later—the vulture disappeared, and there was nothing on the bedposts but the brightly polished brass balls. He knew that he was in bed in the company ranch house; he knew there was a great deal of activity around the place mornings and evenings. Then Bemis and Yates came into his room at dusk, dusty and sweaty and bone-tired.

"You're a danged lazy galoot," Yates said solemnly. "Me and Ed are working our tails off, and you like this bed so well you won't get out of it."

"Tell me what happened, or I'll bend a bedpost over your skull," Scott said in little more than a whisper.

"Ain't he the tough one!" Yates jeered.

"We'll make it quick," Bemis said. "The doc didn't want you bothered on account of you got real friendly with St. Peter for a spell. Seems that Mrs. Schmidt saved your hide. Bengogh was fixing to plug you when you came through the door, and Mrs. Schmidt tangled with him and pushed him down the stairs. She was hysterical for a while, and she told Patsy more'n she aimed to. Seems like she was in love with Bengogh; but, after Alec got plugged, she figured out she was real fond of him."

"Women!" Yates said disgustedly.

"Some way she tricked Bengogh into admitting he'd plugged Alec," Bemis went on, "and then she decided she hated Bengogh. The funny part was that, if Bengogh had waited, he'd have got everything he wanted on account of old Alec had a bad ticker."

"Tally was the one who drilled you, and Hibbard drilled him," Yates said. "Tally lived most of the night. Him and Delazon was outside. They knew you and Hibbard was around, so they waited for you to show in the light; but they heard us coming, and Delazon lost his head. Funny thing about Hibbard. Figured he was a big hero. Handed Runyan his star and said he was leaving the country, now that he'd cleaned everything up."

Perhaps he was a hero, Scott thought. It took real courage for a weak man to prove he was strong when the chips were down. Hibbard might never rise to those same heights again; but this one time he had the right to think of himself as a hero.

"Thought you boys was riding over the hill," Scott said.

Yates grinned blandly. "That was another funny thing. We couldn't find the hill."

"What fetched you out here that night?"

"I don't rightly know," Bemis said thoughtfully. "Nolan and Vance got purty hot after you left. Me and Shorty, too. Or maybe it was Sally who scorched her tongue on Runyan. He was willing enough, at that. Anyhow, some of the boys stayed in town holding their guns on the crew, just to make sure they stayed there, and the rest of us came on, figuring you might need help."

"But that ain't the big news," Yates said expansively. "We got the outfit you wanted. Mrs. Schmidt sold out, lock, stock, and barrel. Won't be no trouble making that drive to Winnemucca now."

"What'd you use for money?"

"Nolan made a quick trip to The Dalles," Bemis answered, "and borrowed all he could. Runyan mortgaged the Triangle R and threw everything he had into the pot. Came out pretty good, everything did."

Sally called from the doorway, "Chuck's ready."

Yates winked at Sally. "You tell him about our iron. Fitting and proper for you to do it."

She came to the bed as Yates and Bemis left the room, and stood looking down at him, her back straight the way he remembered it, her head held high and proud. She was tired, he thought, and thinner, but he saw something in her face that had not been there before—a peace that could come only from a deep inner contentment.

"You were so sick, Scott," she said. "So sick."

"I owe you my life, I reckon." He reached up and took her hand. "I don't savvy, buying this spread. Ain't right, Nolan and your brother being in debt on that account."

"It's exactly right," she told him. "Now we're sure of having peace in the valley. You know how stubborn and careful Jay is. It's good business, or he wouldn't have done it."

"What was that iron Shorty mentioned?"

She flushed. "It was his idea. You see, we're all in a company of our own. You three and Jay and Hank. Your savvy against their money. I'm in it, too. I sold my house."

"What's the iron Shorty was talking about?"

She lowered her gaze, hesitated, and then said, "The S Heart S."

He grinned and pulled her down to him. He kissed her, and for a long moment she pressed her cheek against his, and he knew that he had all her love. He said, "I read somewhere that a man never built anything good without a woman's help. We'll build a spread that'll last forever."

"Where did you read that?" she asked.

"Why, I think it was some old philosopher," he said. "Maybe it was that fellow Plato."

Wayne D. Overholser has won three Golden Spur awards from the Western Writers of America and has a long list of fine Western titles to his credit. He was born in Pomeroy, Washington, and attended the University of Montana, University of Oregon and the University of Southern California before becoming a public school teacher and principal in various Oregon communities. He began writing for Western pulp magazines in 1936 and within a couple of years was a regular contributor to Street & Smith's *Western Story Magazine* and Fiction House's *Lariat Story Magazine*. *Buckaroo's Code* (1947) was his first Western novel and remains one of his best. In the 1950s and 1960s, having retired from academic work to concentrate on writing, he would publish as many as four books a year under his own name or a pseudonym, most prominently as Joseph Wayne. *The Violent Land* (1954), *The Lone Deputy* (1957), and *The Bitter Night* (1961) are among the finest of the early Overholser titles. Overholser's Western novels are based on a solid knowledge of the history and customs of the 19th Century West, particularly when set in his two favorite Western states, Oregon and Colorado. Many of his novels are first person narratives, a technique that tends to bring an added dimension of vividness to the frontier experiences of his narrators and frequently, as in *Cast a Long Shadow* (1957), the female characters one encounters are among the most memorable. He has written his numerous novels with a consistent skill and an uncommon sensitivity to the depths of human character. Almost invariably, his stories weave a spell of their own with their scenes and images of social and economic forces often in conflict and the diverse ways of life and personalities that made the American Western frontier so unique a time and place in human history. *Nugget City* and *Riders of the Sundowns* are his latest books.